MW01617020

# THE WORST RESCUERS IN THE REPUBLIC

## DUMB LUCK AND DEAD HEROES
### BOOK 4

### SKYLER RAMIREZ

# CONTENTS

*To everyone who has ever fallen flat on their face, picked themselves up, and gone on to do incredible things. This story is for you.*

# FOREWORD

Buckle up. Seriously. This one gets wild. It's also longer than the other books in the series. Enjoy!

And don't worry, this is far from the last adventure for Brad and Jessica. There is a lot more to come!

Thanks for Reading,

Skyler Ramirez

# PROLOGUE

### *BRAD MENDOZA*

"**B**rad, you really are stupid, aren't you?"

That is frankly *not* the question a man likes to hear after he's been hanging from his wrists for some unknown number of hours in a small metal room that looks like it hasn't been cleaned in years. And it's especially not a great question coming from a woman you *thought* had the hots for you but actually turned out to be a sadistic killer. Yep, all around, this is a terrible question on a terrible day.

"I mean," continues the woman that I knew as Kayla Carter, "all you have to do to make all this end is give me the coordinates of the stellarium deposit in the Gerson system. Just a few numbers, that's all. I know you have them in your head. Jules told me enough before she was…cut off to know that you're the *only* person who could know them."

She pauses and gives me a sly smile. "Besides, what do you care if we find it? You gave King Charles your entire life, and how did he repay you? By declaring you a fugitive so that you had to fake your own death, that's how. So why not just give me the coordinates, and we can put this whole nasty business behind us?"

She stops, waiting for my reply. When I first met Kayla, I thought she looked cute in that girl-next-door kind of way. She has an innocent face with a small nose surrounded by freckles under messy blond hair. And she's so short and petite that no one would ever peg her as a ruthless mercenary leader. But here we are, and now she just looks like a psycho, mostly because that's exactly what she is.

"Excuse me, Miss," I say, "I'd really love to talk to your manager or the concierge. My room has no fresh bedding, and the blood stains on the walls are a real concern for me. One star out of five; would not recommend."

Kayla's smile disappears, and she sneers and shakes her head at me. "Brad, Brad, Brad, always with a joke. You know, I usually don't enjoy torturing people, but I think your case will be an exception."

"I don't know," I say flippantly. "Nothing can be more torture than listening to you blather on."

Her sneer turns into a snarl, and she moves her arm like lightning, the back of her hand connecting with my cheek, and I feel a wetness on my face. She pulls back her hand to strike again, and I brace myself, but I'm saved by the sound of the small room's only hatch opening.

Of course, I find myself wishing little Kayla had taken the time to get a few more hits in so it would delay what I see now. The man I knew as Norman Smith—the one who posed as the militia leader for Carter's World—walks in pushing a cart loaded with what looks like a large battery and jumper cables.

Kayla smiles almost sweetly again, though the rest of her face still conveys the anger of seconds ago. "Brad, Sweetheart, I'm going to leave you with Jerod here and let him teach you the cost of playing dumb with me. Whenever you're ready to make it stop, you just scream out those coordinates, and maybe we'll even let you live."

With that, she turns and walks briskly out of the room without a backward glance, leaving me with a way-too-happy-looking Norman—Jerod. As I watch her go, what little hope I had goes with her. She just told me Norman's real name, which means that no matter what I tell them, they are *never* planning to let me go alive.

# ONE
## PAIN

*JESSICA LIN*

I don't know how long I've been asleep. I vaguely remember waking up before this, though I can't recall anything of substance from those semi-lucid moments. But I do remember one thing: the pain. It's here with me now, so harsh and demanding that I can't ignore it, and even though I fight not to wake up and face it, it's so insistent that I have no choice but to let it drag me out of unconsciousness.

My eyes flutter open, and then I immediately squeeze them shut again. It's so *bright*. I keep them shut tightly for a few moments, and then I crack one eye just barely and then the other. Little by little, I open them more as they adjust, to find myself staring at a stark white ceiling with lights that I now recognize as actually being quite dim.

"Jessica, you're awake!" I hear a male voice exclaim, and then a familiar face enters my view. It's Harris. And with his face, the memories come flooding back:

A comm call with Brad, telling him about my father's betrayal.

Harris screaming about detecting a bomb on board our ship.

My frantic race to find the bomb and eject it from the airlock.

The massive explosion just as I closed the inner airlock hatch.

Waking up on fire and...Harris carrying me as everything went black.

Brad!

"Brad!" I try to scream out loud, but it comes out only as a painful hacking cough that burns as bad as everything else I'm feeling now.

"Nurse! Nurse!" I hear Harris yell just above my choking cries, and a sturdy woman appears a moment later carrying a very large needle, which she sticks into a tube I didn't notice before. But it's the last thing I see before sleep takes me again.

# TWO
## WAKING UP

**_JESSICA LIN_**

"Miss Lin, can you hear me?"

I fight to open my eyes—they're just so heavy for some reason—and find myself in the same white room I woke up in before. The pain is lessened now, though I can still feel it, lurking just outside my senses, as if it's waiting to rush in and assault me again.

A face I've never seen before peers down at me in a clinical fashion, and I open my mouth in a question that won't come out. Even the attempt to force air out of my lungs to speak brings a sharp spike of intrusion from the waiting pain.

"Miss Lin, don't try to speak. I'm Doctor Wellesley. You gave us quite a scare. Blink, please, if you can understand me."

7

I comply, and the doctor nods. "Terrific. We were able to repair the worst of the damage to your lungs and esophagus, but the more you rest them, the faster you'll be able to resume speaking again. Blink if you understand me.

I blink again.

"That's good, very good, Miss Lin. Do you know where you are? Blink once for yes, twice for no."

I think for a moment, turning my eyes to try and see more of the room I'm in, but the walls are as white and nondescript as the ceiling. All I can tell for sure is that I'm not on my ship—or any other ship, for that matter —I can't feel the vibrations that would usually be a dead giveaway for an operating spacecraft. Listening and feeling for them has become so instinctual to me over the years that even in my foggy state, their absence is as loud to me as someone shouting in my ear.

I blink twice.

The doctor smiles thinly. "I suspected as much. This isn't the first time you've been awake, but you were barely with us the last few times. You almost died twice, in fact. You're through the worst of it now, though there will be a long road to recovery, I'm afraid."

No! The doctor's words send a panic through me, and I involuntarily try to sit up, only to find that I can't move any of my limbs. That causes my panic to ratchet up several levels, and I start hyperventilating and trying to speak despite the doctor's orders, though all I can seem to force out of my mouth is a high-pitched keening sound.

I have to get up! I have to get up! I have to get up!

The doctor disappears and reappears with a needle. My eyes lock on it in horror. But this time, when it's injected into my IV line, the darkness doesn't come. Instead, I feel my muscles relax suddenly and drastically.

"Sorry," the man says, "but I can't have you struggling and hurting yourself further. You have third-degree burns on over a third of your body, and I'm afraid we don't have the facilities here to do more than stabilize you and treat the burns. We cannot, unfortunately, repair the cosmetic damage."

I look up at him, so relaxed now that I'm not even able to open my mouth to try to speak again, and instead try to convey a question through my eyes.

Either he gets it or was about to give me the answer anyway. "What I mean to say, Miss Lin is that we'll be able to return you to more-or-less normal movement and stave off any infection. But you'll be scarred and disfigured until you can get yourself to a facility with skin regen capabilities. Other than that, you'll be fine in about two weeks and ready to be discharged."

My mind is moving slower now from whatever drug he gave me, so it takes me a few seconds to process his words and grasp their meaning. When I finally do, I feel tears spring to my eyes. The doctor sees them and misinterprets their cause.

"I know that this must come as a shock to you, but the scars *will* be repairable. Like I said, you'll just need to get care in a system that can regen the skin. That whole process takes a while but can be done largely as an outpatient procedure. In fact…"

He continues to prattle on, giving me assurances that I'll look 'normal' again. But I find myself not caring about any of that. No, what hits me hardest is that he said I'll have to be here for another two full *weeks*. And I'm not sure Brad has that long.

# THREE
# UNHEALTHY CO-DEPENDENCIES

## *BRAD MENDOZA*

I awake slowly, finding myself still in the little metal room, though at least now I'm just lying huddled on the hard metal grate deck instead of hanging from the ceiling by my wrists. That's an improvement, I suppose.

I hear footsteps on the metal deck outside my room —probably what woke me—and lift my head up just as the room's hatch itself swings slowly inward. I groan as I recognize the short and thin figure of Kayla backlit in the brighter light from the corridor outside.

Briefly, I consider getting to my feet and lunging at her, but I'm just so *tired* in every way. Besides, my wrists are bound with thick cords, and an experimental movement of my feet reveals the same for my ankles.

So, I just watch her enter the room and close the

hatch behind her, stopping for a moment to let her eyes adjust to the dimmer light in my cell. To my bemusement, she's not wearing her typical garb, what I've come to think of as her 'evil mercenary outfit'. Instead of the black skinsuit with body armor on top, she's dressed as she was when I first met her, wearing a pair of cutoff jean shorts, a thin white t-shirt, and a red flannel. She's not wearing any shoes, and she tip-toes carefully across the room to me and crouches down in front of me, reaching out a hand toward my face.

I recoil back, though doing so sends shooting pain through every muscle in my body, and Kayla actually looks hurt for a second. But she doesn't give up, reaching out further toward me and…

…stroking my hair gently.

"Oh, Brad," she says in a husky voice. "I hate to see you suffering so much. You have to understand, *I* don't want to do this. But my employers…well, they insist on it. And if I don't do as they demand, they'll kill us both. No, if it were up to me, we'd approach this so much differently. I like you, Brad, I really do. What I felt for you on *Wanderer* and on Carter's World, that was *real*. You believe me, don't you?"

I fight not to roll my eyes. Does she really think I'm that stupid or that *desperate*? Sure, in SERE training, when they taught Promethean officers how to resist interrogation, they talked about Stockholm Syndrome and interrogators using false love as a form of incentive to get prisoners talking. But Kayla's poor attempt now is just so pathetic.

"Brad," she continues, maybe reading my lack of response as interest, "let's run away together. You and me; we can give my employers what they want, then we can take the credits and live somewhere happily ever after. You'd like that, wouldn't you?"

This time, I *do* roll my eyes, but there's a clang in the corridor outside the room, and Kayla turns to regard the hatch, missing my expression of disgust. When she turns back, she looks frightened.

"Brad. They're coming. Quick, tell me you'll do it. Tell me you'll give me the coordinates so we can run away together...so we can *be* together. Hurry before the rest of these mercenaries figure out what I'm doing in here."

"Come here," I whisper, just low enough that I doubt she can hear me. She looks puzzled and leans down toward me.

"Closer," I say, and this time, I know she can hear me because her face takes on a brief look of excitement. She thinks I'm cracking. Kayla leans down within centimeters of my face.

"The coordinates are..." I start and am gratified by her leaning even closer and turning her head so that one ear is practically pressed to my lips. And that's when I spit right in that ear. It's a great glob of spit with a little mucus and snot mixed in. Some of my best work.

Kayla shoots to her feet, shrieking in disgust and frustration and reaching up with one hand to frantically wipe at her ear with the cuff of her flannel. As she does so, the hatch behind her clangs open, and an older man steps in, alarm on his face. He takes in the scene quickly and, seeing that Kayla is in no physical danger from me, relaxes just a tad.

"I take it he didn't give up the coordinates?" the

man I knew as President Carter asks as he shuts the hatch behind him. He moves up to stand next to Kayla, staring down at me with a sneer.

She looks over at him with an expression I've seen many women use when a man says something painfully obvious. Carla used that expression with me pretty often, even back when I hadn't drunk myself into stupidity. But Carter, as I still think of him, ignores her acidic look and puts an arm around her, his hand coming to rest in a place that shows they are *definitely* not father and daughter as they originally purported to be.

I can't help myself. I laugh, even though they both loom over me as I lay helpless on the floor. "Seriously?" I ask. "You and him? But he's so…*old*. I mean, I knew you have daddy issues, Kayla, but this is ridiculous!"

The last thing I see is the man's black boot descending toward my face.

# FOUR
# A SHIP AND A CREW

*JESSICA LIN*

True to the doctor's word, it takes me two full weeks to recover enough to move normally and be able to do so without heavy pain relievers. But the day I finally get out of the hospital, I'm ready to charge to the capital city's shuttle port and demand passage up to their orbital and my waiting ship. Add in the four days I was largely out cold, and Brad's kidnappers have a bit more than a two-and-a-half week head start on us. I need to get going now!

But instead, a day later, I'm sitting on the front porch of what is perhaps the most serene place I've ever been. Like the place that the fake Kayla Carter took us to, this is also a farm. But unlike that other farm, this one has animals roaming the fields and young men and women out working. I watch now as a man in his early twenties rides a barely broken horse around a small enclosure, the sweat gleaming off the large animal's flanks as the man puts it through its paces.

It reminds me of when I was a girl and my mother insisted I take riding lessons. Only that was in a shiny facility with English saddles and hard riding helmets. In contrast, the scene in front of me now makes that modern equestrian center on Prometheus feel like a manufactured environment; what I see here on Carter's World is somehow raw by comparison, but that only makes it feel all the more real.

Despite its beauty, I hate it. There's only one place I want to be right now and one thing I want to be doing, and it involves getting my hands around Kayla Carter's neck—or whatever her real name is.

"Nice to see you out of bed," a gruff older man's voice says from behind me. I turn gingerly in the wooden rocking chair and force a wan smile at the broad figure of President Frank Carter—the *real* President Carter. He's taller than Brad, with broad shoulders that taper into a midsection that, despite his seventy years of age, shows only a small paunch. The president is wearing worn jeans and a flannel shirt and looks very unpresidential. But the lines on his face speak of someone who smiles a lot, and if that's unpresidential, then we should have more men like him in positions of power.

It pains me that I'm about to put a frown on that face, but by the wary look in his eyes, I can tell he's not here to give me good news.

"How is *Persephone*?" I ask, easing into the difficult conversation.

He smiles. "Your ship is spaceworthy. We may not have a full-fledged shipyard or even an adequate repair dock, but we do have a bunch of folks who know how to weld on hull plates. Your ship will fly, at least until you can get it to a proper shipyard for a better repair job."

I smile my appreciation as he lowers himself into the rocking chair next to me; the slow way in which he does so is the first real sign of his advanced age on a planet that doesn't have the rejuvenation treatments that are common even on a Fringe capital like Prometheus.

The first time I met Frank Carter was just a few hours after my first conversation—at least the first one I remember—with Doctor Wellesley. The President visited me in the hospital, asking what I wanted in return for saving his planet and system from the pirate threat. I got the impression I could have asked for just about anything, but I only pressed him for two things, though neither was a particularly small request. It's nice to know he honored the first one, fixing my ship.

"And the other thing I asked for?" I say, expecting I won't like this answer.

He frowns, confirming my suspicion. "Now, Miss Lin. I'm grateful for what you and your captain did here. Heck, we all are. We owe you a pretty piece for ridding us of Poulter and his crew. But my planet is hurting. We haven't had a decent export in a year, and we're in need of all sorts of medicine and other goods we can't make ourselves. If I give you the funds you're talking about, a lot of my people will suffer more than they even are now. And I just can't countenance that. I hope you understand."

A dozen protests rise to my lips. The hardest part is that I *do* understand, and I even agree with him. But I'm going to argue anyway, because I can't let myself care as much as he does about *his* people, when *my* people—my captain—is being held somewhere waiting on me to rescue him.

"Mr. President," I begin to argue. "What I'm asking is only fair. And while I sympathize with your plight, Captain Mendoza didn't ask to be kidnapped by mercenaries when he was liberating your system. It's only fair that you…"

"Now, now, Miss Lin," he says, holding up a hand to forestall further argument. "I said I can't give you what you *asked* for, but I think maybe I can give you the next best thing."

I furrow my brows together. I wish I could raise just one, like Brad does. I've always envied people who can do that. It conveys so much in a single expression. But I think I'm still getting my skepticism across pretty well, even if one side of my face doesn't actually have an eyebrow anymore.

Despite all that, Carter smiles kindly. "Now let's see," he says almost absently, turning his gaze out over the farm and away from me, "they should be arriving right about now."

"Who?" I ask, turning my gaze with his toward the farm's long front drive, wincing at the feeling of still unhealed skin stretching in my neck and upper chest as I do so. When I finally face the right direction, I can see an old-fashioned wheeled car approaching in a cloud of dust.

Carter doesn't answer my question but just sits there, watching the car with that almost infuriating smile on his face.

A car turns into the small yard in front of the house, parking between the farmhouse and the barn. I watch as four people, two men and two women, get out. They're all wearing what looks like some sort of uniform, green with gold trim, though the clothing has the same rough, homespun look as everything else I've seen on this planet.

All four of them walk up to the house and the railing that separates the porch upon which Carter and I sit from the dusty yard. They draw up and give a smart salute to President Carter and then settle into an at-ease stance without being told.

"Commander Lin," President Carter says, using my old Navy rank for the first time, "allow me to introduce you to Commander Illian, Lieutenant Robinson, Chief Perry, and Chief Jensen. They're the senior remaining folks from our system patrol crew, the alternate crew that wasn't on rotation when we fought Poulter's pirates. But each one of them was listening from the ops center when their colleagues died. As you can imagine, that left quite an impression on them."

I nod respectfully at the men and women in front of us, but I say nothing. I know what Carter is trying to do; he wants to stir up my sympathy for his planet so that I'll drop my demands and leave with what he's already given me. But I can't do that. I have to stay the course, or I'll have no hope of getting Brad back. I prepare myself to say something to that effect when one of the men, Commander Illian, steps forward.

"Ma'am—Commander," he says, nodding to me. "We would like to respectfully offer you our services on board your ship. We have petitioned President Carter, and he has granted us three months of paid leave to join you on your mission…if you'll have us."

The subtle rebuke I was planning for Carter dies on my lips as I look at the commander in surprise and then over at Carter. The old dog has a sly grin on his face now, and I'm almost positive he knows exactly what I was thinking before Illian spoke.

"I…" but I'm not sure what to say and find myself trailing off.

"They've all volunteered, every one of the twelve men and women under Commander Illian," Carter says. "In fact, about half of them threatened to resign from our system patrol—such as it is—if I didn't let them go with you."

"But I thought you'd need them to crew that captured pirate vessel," I find myself protesting. I may have taken the pirate corvette for my own, but there was one more ship, a smaller patrol boat, left out at that pirate base. And as far as the planetary sensors can tell, it's still there, or so Carter has told me.

He shrugs. "That's what I told them. But, well, I think I can spare them for a few months. Probably take that long just to save up enough to fuel the darn thing anyway. And since I'm already paying them, it seems they ought to be doing something to earn that pay. I figure with you, at least they'll get good training and experience."

Despite his words about the benefits to him and his world, I can see past all that. The president knows that he's giving me a gift; the entire reason I wanted the money from his world for services rendered was to be able to find and hire a crew. But Carter just saved me the money *and* time it would take to do so.

"Thank you," I say simply, sensing that to be any more effusive might actually annoy the old man. "I accept."

"Ma'am," one of the uniformed women steps forward, Chief Perry, I believe. She's older, probably in her late fifties. "If it's all right with you, we can have the rest of the crew mustered and on the orbital this time tomorrow."

"That will be fine, Chief," I say somberly, trying hard to suppress the emotional response that's churning in my guts at this unexpected gift. "I suppose I'll meet you there."

## FIVE
# ALL DRESSED UP AND NOWHERE TO GO

### *JESSICA LIN*

"Captain, course set for the jump point and engines at flank speed," Chief Jensen tells me from the helm station on *Persephone*'s small bridge. Despite my new *Persephone* being a corvette, about eighty percent the tonnage of her namesake frigate—of which all that remains is scattered wreckage back in Gerson—the bridge I sit on now is actually larger than I would expect, with duty stations for five officers and spacers, including the commander, whereas my old ship only had room for four.

"Thank you, Chief," I say, "but in the future, you will refer to me as 'Commander.' I'm not the captain of this ship; that's who we're on our way to save."

"Yes, Ma'am…uh, Commander," Jensen says sheepishly, and I find myself almost wishing he would argue. Lieutenant Junior-Grade Petra Yesayan from the old *Persephone* would have argued, spouting naval regulations that the commanding officer on any ship, regardless of rank, is to always be referred to as 'Captain'. But Jensen doesn't cite regulations at me or argue in any other way.

Unfortunately, that's how this entire new crew of mine has been acting since they first came on board yesterday. It still kills me that we wasted an entire day, but it was unavoidable; they had to familiarize themselves with the ship, after all. For all of that, their learning curve has been especially impressive. They seem to have taken to the unfamiliar Koratan systems like they've been using them all their lives. From what I can tell, the long-lost captain of their patrol ship, who died in the battle with Poulter, was more than competent, and she transferred that competence to each and every one of her small, two-rotation crew.

Unfortunately, there is *one* area they haven't managed to learn as quickly as I'd like. I keep telling them that *I'm* not their captain on *Persephone*. I'm the XO; I'm just keeping Brad's seat warm until he gets back. But no matter how many times I remind them of that fact, they just keep calling me 'Captain'. Frankly, I don't care that naval regulations and tradition support them in this; I'm not in the Navy anymore, so I don't have to follow their rules anymore either. Still, my crew doesn't seem to be getting the message.

Add to that the fact that they seem doggedly intent on hero-worshipping me. They won't argue with anything I say, even if they might have a better suggestion. Rather, they seem to accept it as an article of faith that I know what I'm doing.

If only they knew…

"Ahem," comes the sound of a throat clearing behind me. There is one member of my new crew who neither worships me nor shows any fear whatsoever of talking back to me. I turn now and regard Chief Winoma Perry, the oldest member of my new crew. She's wearing a frown and has her eyebrows raised at me expectantly. "It's time, Commander," she says in a no-nonsense tone.

I wilt. "Really? Didn't we just do that?"

She frowns the way my mother used to when I argued about going to martial arts lessons, riding lessons, etiquette lessons, or the myriad of other never-ending lessons she used to send me to. "Every four hours while you're awake," Perry says.

"But we're just leaving port," I argue, sounding whiny even to my own ears. Luckily, the rest of the bridge crew pretends not to notice.

By the look on Winoma Perry's face, she's not amused nor dissuaded. She manages to convey with just her eyes that I had better come willingly, or she'll take me not-so-willingly.

"Fine. Commander Illian, you have the conn," I say to my…he thinks he's my executive officer, but *I'm* the executive officer on this boat, so he's my tactical officer. He nods briskly and moves around from the tactical station to take up the command chair as I painfully lever myself out of it to follow my torturer into my day cabin.

Suddenly, my knees go weak. Thinking of Perry as

my torturer, even in jest, just sent my brain to a very dark place that I've mostly forced myself to avoid the last three weeks: the thought of the *real* torture Brad is undoubtedly enduring right this moment.

Luckily, Illian is there to catch me under one arm and keep me from slumping to the deck. The rest of the crew watches in stunned silence as he picks me up and holds my arm until I can steady myself again. Then he glares at the rest of them.

"What?" he asks. "Let's see if any of you can get blown up and, three weeks later, command a warship."

By the looks on the faces of all of them, they aren't actually judging me—I almost wish they were—instead, their expressions brim over with sympathy and…anger. But not anger at me, but rather at those who did this to me. Their new…captain. Somehow, that sympathy and anger hurt worse than if they were really just judging me.

All this passes through my head quickly before I tear my eyes away from them and follow Chief Perry through the door into my small day cabin—well, Brad's small day cabin; I'm just using it until we find him.

Perry shuts the hatch behind me as I lower myself onto the room's small couch, my legs still trembling. Misreading, as Illian did, the cause of my weak state, she frowns down at me.

"Doctor Wellesley told you to take it easy, Commander," she chides. "Commander Illian is fully capable of conning the ship to the jump point and beyond if you'd tell us where we're headed after that."

I lower my face, worried that she'll see the hot tears forming there. I fail at hiding them, and her tone

26

suddenly switches from that of a scolding mother to a sympathetic grandmother.

"Now look here, Commander Lin, there will be none of that. You're not alone in this, but the sooner you let us in on your plan, the sooner we can take some of this tremendous load off your shoulders. That's what a crew is for." I expect her to tack 'young lady' to the end of that sentence, but she doesn't, and I'm thankful for it.

"That's just it, Chief," I confess, "I have no idea where they've taken Brad—Captain Mendoza—so I have no plan yet. I don't know even where to start."

I hear a slurping sound and look up to see her squirting a large dollop of lotion into her hand from a bottle she's produced out of nowhere. I wince but almost mechanically stand up and unzip my skinsuit, stepping out of it and standing there shivering in front of the woman.

"Of course, you don't know where to start," she chides as she walks around to my back and starts to lather on the lotion that's supposed to both help my burns heal and keep the scars softened enough that they won't fully impede my motion, at least until I can get them fixed permanently. I get to go through this every four hours during the day and wake up and do it at least once every night. To add to the indignity, I can't reach a healthy portion of the scars, especially those on my back, so I need help with the horrible little ritual.

"I imagine this is the first time you've had to save your captain, or anyone else for that matter, from mercenary kidnappers hell-bent on evading you?"

I nod, but she continues, not waiting for a response, which is good because I don't trust my voice right now.

Not only am I an emotional wreck, but I wince and hiss every time she adds more lotion; the stuff *really* stings.

"But lucky for you," she says, "you aren't doing this alone. And because you don't know where they've taken him, you can't know in any case where we *should* go next. So pick a direction and a system because when there's no way to know the right answer, there's no wrong answers either."

I consider her words, but I'm not sure if they're deep or ridiculous. She moves around to my front now and starts spreading the lotion liberally across the burned half of my stomach, stopping where the scars disappear under my undergarments. The first time she did this, she told me to take those off as well, but I drew a hard line on that. Some things I *can* do for myself.

"You see, Commander," she says, "assuming that horrible Kayla person and her crew operate normally in this part of the Fringe, there's apt to be someone who knows of her in just about any station or orbital we come across."

The logic actually makes sense, and I want to slap myself for committing the classic folly of overthinking the problem; I'm guilty of that a lot. Perry finishes on my stomach and neck and then moves down to do my left leg, which is burned almost entirely down to my ankle. I suck in a breath as the lotion hits a particularly raw spot behind my knee.

Finished, Perry stands up and hands me the lotion bottle, meeting my eyes levelly, though she's about five centimeters shorter than I am. "Commander, what I'm trying to say is that any decision is better than no decision. So, make a decision, and we'll follow."

I nod, still not trusting my voice, and take the lotion bottle from her. She leaves out the opposite hatch into the corridor outside so that no one still on the bridge will see me in all my burned and scarred glory. When the hatch closes behind her, I slowly and painfully start the work of rubbing the lotion into my face and other regions that I don't let Perry do for me. And somehow, the repetitive motion and even the sting of the lotion soothe my mind as I slowly start to think through my next step.

When I return to the bridge, Commander Illian briskly hops out of the captain's chair and returns to the tactical station. I look over to see that, at some point, Harris wandered onto the bridge. He's been a constant at my side since the explosion that almost killed me, and I smile warmly at him now. He smiles back encouragingly. For all the grief Brad liked to give the guy, Harris is an extremely steady crewmember and…friend, I suppose.

"Chief Jensen," I say with no hint of my near-emotional-breakdown in my voice, "please calculate the fastest jump paths to get us to the Fiori system."

To one side, I see Illian raise an inquisitive eyebrow —just one, and it reminds me of Brad and almost sends me spiraling again. "That's a four-day journey at flank speed, Commander," he says. "What's at Fiori?"

I ignore his direct question. "Commander Illian, when you don't know where your prey is now, you go where they *will* be later."

He nods, understanding. "And you have reason to believe the kidnappers will take Captain Mendoza to Fiori."

I shake my head, wincing as it pulls at the still-healing skin on the left side of my neck and chest. "No, Commander. I suspect that what they want is in Gerson, though Fiori is roughly on the way there."

"I see," he responds. "Then what, if I may ask, is at Fiori?"

I turn and regard him, but not with annoyance. He's asking the questions because that's what a good executive officer—which I suppose he is, even if only temporarily—does, and his tone carries no doubt or challenge, only genuine curiosity. I can see why he rose to the rank he's at, which is, somewhat awkwardly, that of a full commander, a rank above my Promethean station as a lieutenant commander.

"There's something—someone, really—at Fiori who I think may be able to help us find where the mercenaries who took Captain Mendoza are hiding now."

Illian smiles, obviously relieved to hear that there's an actual plan, though he can't know yet just how incomplete and weak that plan really is. "And will this person help us willingly?" he asks.

It's my turn to smile at him. "Not if we're lucky."

## SIX
# BATTERY CABLES

### *BRAD MENDOZA*

**H**ave you ever had battery cables attached to your most sensitive bits? I can't recommend it; it *really* hurts. Even when the battery itself isn't connected, the metal teeth of the clamps themselves aren't exactly what I would call comfortable. And now, Jerod—the guy I knew as Norman Smith—is taking it one step further by pressing a button on a small handheld control that closes a connection and sends who knows how much electricity coursing through those bits.

I scream; I can't help it. The agony that shoots through my entire body as it spasms and clenches is beyond words and seems to last for an eternity before he releases the button, and I slump back in utter exhaustion into the chair they've tied me to.

31

"You know, Brad," Jerod says, his tone conversational, "it was fun to watch you—a Navy squid—try and teach my experienced ground pounders how to be soldiers on Carter's World. When in reality, any one of us could have taken that gun and that smug look on your face away from you and given you a *real* lesson in what it means to be a soldier."

He presses the button, and I arch my back and scream again, then slump back once more as he releases it.

I take a few ragged breaths and then force air out to talk. "What could they have shown me? How to assault a nursery school or subdue an old woman. I'm sorry, Norm, but the level of incompetence they showed those first few days is something you just can't fake. I mean—"

My words turn into a meaningless scream as he ups the voltage and presses the button again.

"Always have to have the last word, don't you, Brad?" he sneers. "Well, Kayla told me I get you for the entire afternoon, so you and I are going to have all the time we want to discuss the finer points of infantry tactical doctrine."

He releases the button and lets me collapse again in my restraints. Then he sets the evil little button down on the cart that contains the really big battery I'm hooked up to and takes a step forward, crouching down so he can look me in the eye.

"You want to know the difference between Kayla and me, Brad? She's torturing you because she wants those coordinates. Me? I'm torturing you mainly because I just *really* don't like you. Talking down to me like you did on Carter's World...I wanted to just kill you then. But if I had, I would have deprived myself of these fun little sessions. So, you feel free just to keep those coordinates to yourself. It just means more quality time together."

"Norm," I say between gasping breaths, "you might want to talk to someone about your... anger... management... issues." I run out of breath there at the end, which totally spoils the jab, but his face still twists in rage, proving my point, really, and he steps back, picking up the button again.

"Let's turn up the voltage again, shall we, Brad?"

I shrug as much as I can in my restraints. "Sure. It kind of tickles."

When he presses the button next, I immediately regret poking the very angry bear.

# SEVEN

# A NEW RECRUIT...A BIG ONE

*JESSICA LIN*

The new crew I got for Brad is amazing, and I'll be eternally grateful to the real President Carter for loaning them to me and even keeping them on his planet's payroll for hopefully long enough for us to find and rescue our captain.

But despite how wonderful they are, they're spacers, not soldiers. If I'm going to have a prayer of rescuing Brad, I'm going to need some Marines—or whatever the mercenary equivalent is.

I mean, *I* can fight. My single mother had the same healthy level of paranoia about her daughter's safety as most women mistreated by the world have. But with what my father sent us—once she grudgingly accepted it—she had far more money to address those fears than the average single mother. So, in addition to the riding lessons, sports, dance, and other activities she practically forced me to endure, she also enrolled me in martial arts at a young age. And while I tolerated most of the extracurricular activities to make her happy, I *loved* taekwondo.

They awarded me my second-degree black belt just before I enrolled in the Naval Academy. There, I quickly became the champion of the women's hand-to-hand combat division. I even fought several of the highest-ranked men in exhibition matches and only lost to three of them. There's not much in life I actually consider myself good at, but when it comes to fighting without weapons, I'm *great*.

But Kayla has at least twenty men and women, all hardened fighters, on her crew. And they're heavily armed, having gotten away with all that remained of the weapons in *Wanderer's* hold when they took Brad and the ship. I have a pistol and the one assault rifle I grabbed from that weapons store before I went tearing in after Brad to back him up against Poulter and his goons; that's it. So, I need people who can fight and who can preferably bring their own armament. Because no matter how good I may be at hand-to-hand combat, a guy with a gun will beat me every time.

Which—along with my desire to stall what I know I need to do next—is why I'm currently sitting in a smoky station bar in the Fiori system, across the table from a huge black man who is drinking beer from a glass that looks comically small in his massive hand.

I haven't had the best experience of late with large

men. Most recently was Tucker, Owen Thompson's thug, who made my skin crawl every time he looked at me. And before that was Petty Officer Nedrin Jacobs, who...I shudder involuntarily. I don't even want to *think* about Jacobs. I keep the thoughts of him and all he and my former captain, Jessup, did to me locked away tight in a dark corner of my brain that I almost never allow myself to visit. But seeing this big guy across from me threatens to unlock that mental strongbox and bring forth emotions I've worked very hard to suppress, and I have to remind myself that I asked *him* for this meeting.

He sets down his beer and studies me carefully. I brace myself to endure another man's leering gaze, even though the hood I'm wearing mostly covers my face and I'm in loose clothing because my skinsuit was chafing my burns horribly. Because, in my experience, most men can and *will* look past all that and still imagine what I look like underneath. But, to my surprise, this man, Quinn Boyd, doesn't look at me like that at all, and I have the distinct impression that he's not studying me as a woman but that he's assessing me as a potential threat. It's oddly refreshing.

"How'd you get the scars?" he asks, his low baritone voice a pleasant rumble that reminds me of my Taekwondo master when I was a child.

Still, I frown as I pull back the hood and reveal my face in the light. I was really hoping *not* to have my disfigurement be the center of conversation.

"My ship; there was a bomb on board," I tell him honestly.

He nods. "Looks like C8; I'd say about six ounces.

You were probably on the other side of a closed hatch or bulkhead from it when it blew."

My eyes involuntarily go wide. "How?"

He shrugs. "I like bombs. They're kind of my thing. I can tell from the burn pattern, or what's visible, at least. C8 burns hot and fast, so the hard line between what's burned and what isn't is a dead giveaway. As for the rest, you're sitting here alive, which you wouldn't be if you'd been in the same room as the thing. And anything more than six ounces going off *inside* a ship would have done enough damage to anything smaller than a destroyer so that, again, you wouldn't be sitting here alive."

Now, it's my turn to give *him* an appraising look, and I find myself unexpectedly liking what I see. He's huge, to begin with—not as big as Tucker, but bigger than…the other guy I don't want to think about. But he's got the manner about him of a gentle giant. Still, he reminds me of several Marines I've served with, and my guess is that, like them, he can go from gentle giant to unstoppable wall of death and terror at the drop of a helmet.

"So, what's the job?" Quinn asks casually as he picks up his beer and takes another sip. My own drink still sits in front of me, untouched.

"A friend of mine was kidnapped by mercenaries," I say, deciding to take the risk of trusting this man. After all, I sought *him* out, though in a very ordinary way. I was perusing a screen of classified ads in the station's main concourse and saw his name listed next to the words 'security expert', which I figured correctly was just another way of saying 'mercenary soldier'.

He nods as if friends getting kidnapped by mercenaries is a daily event for him. "Well, my team and I, we specialize in that sort of thing. But we're not cheap. And we're in high demand."

I raise my eyebrows, or at least the one I have left. "Really? Because I only commed you an hour ago, and here you are." I say the words cautiously, knowing I likely can't afford to pay whatever he normally charges, so I have to negotiate, but also recognizing that—martial arts training or not—this guy could break me in half if he so chooses.

To my relief, he grins. "Yeah, guess you got me on that one. But still, I have certain minimum rates. And my team comes as a package deal: all or nothing. There's six of us, and you pay for all six."

My relief deepens; his loyalty to his team speaks well of him, and I will definitely need more than one shooter to rescue Brad. But then my momentary optimism disappears because I'm sure I can't afford him *alone*, much less his five teammates.

"How much?" I ask, knowing that I should *probably* name a number first but afraid that I'll insult him by offering far too little and end the conversation now.

He blows air through his nose in a short laugh. "New at this, aren't you? Well, seeing that, as you pointed out, I'm not exactly beating off employers with a stick right now, twenty thousand per month for me and my team."

My heart sinks. I have exactly eight thousand to my name after Carter bought from me some of the loot I'd taken from Poulter's base. And while I still have *some* of that bounty locked away in a storage closet on board

*Persephone*, it's not as if I know the first thing about fencing stolen goods.

Boyd must notice my fallen expression because he actually takes on a sympathetic look. "Listen, why don't you tell me how much you can offer, and we'll see how far apart we are?"

I hesitate, knowing that he's almost certainly going to walk away. But, nothing ventured, nothing gained. "Four thousand," I tell him, my voice small. "Upfront," I quickly add before he can get up, "and I expect the mercenaries we go after to have more we can take from them. It's a long story, but we took down a pirate base with them—before we even knew they were mercenaries—and they took the lion's share of the loot while we took the bigger ship as our prize."

This is it; I know it. This is where Quinn Boyd stands up and walks away, probably laughing at my lowball offer. But instead, his gaze sharpens. "Wait. You the ones who took out Poulter's base out in that hick system beyond the Collective? Carter's Planet or something like that?"

I nod, surprised.

Quinn grins widely. "If you were actually drinking, I'd buy you another round. Poulter killed a cousin of mine a few years back." He leans back in his seat now, and I can tell he's thinking hard. "Why don't you tell me the entire story, front to back, and we'll see what's possible?"

Later, it will probably shock me how readily I agree. And before I know it, I've told him *everything*, from the time Brad and I met Kayla to the moment we figured out something was off and my ship exploded. I even tell him our true identities and about being on the run from my old Navy and being—sort of—dead. He listens attentively the entire time, asking a few questions here and there but otherwise letting me tell the tale. When I'm done, he downs the rest of his beer in a quick gulp and practically slams the glass down on the table between us, causing me to jump.

"Well, isn't that something? And a corvette? I wondered who owned that little warship docked out there, but I should have guessed right off the bat, given the obvious explosive damage. Looks like someone peeled open the starboard airlock with a can opener.

"Listen, tell you what. You agree to cut me and my team in for half the loot when we take out those mercenaries and rescue your captain and give us that four thousand you promised, and we'll take the job."

My heart leaps in my chest, and I'm about to happily exclaim a definitive 'yes!' but I stop myself. "A third of the loot. I have my crew to consider," I tell him.

He grins again. "For the woman who killed Poulter, done." I actually told him the truth, that Kayla herself killed Poulter, but I don't argue with his giving me the credit.

"Now," he says, "you may not be drinking, but I am. And while I drink my next beer, tell me what you know so far about where your captain is."

"Well," I say sheepishly, "that's the tricky part. I *don't* know, but I think there's someone in this system who will. I hope."

When I tell him the name, he almost drops his beer,

and I half expect him to walk away for real this time. But instead, he gets weirdly excited and starts brainstorming with me ways to get to the man we're targeting. By the end of the conversation and his third beer, I'm finding that I very much like Quinn Boyd.

## EIGHT
# SHEDDING WATER

### JESSICA LIN

"You're serious?" Commander Illian asks incredulously, losing his customary professional tone for a moment as we sit at *Persephone's* small wardroom table. With us are Lieutenant Robinson, a tall, willowy woman, and Lieutenant Jericho, the final of the three living system patrol officers from Carter's World and my current chief engineer. Chief Perry is also there, as the senior enlisted, frowning at me in her customary way.

We're all seated around the small table, but Quinn Boyd, the last person in the room, leans up against the closed hatch. The man is literally too big to fit between the table and its fixed benches, so he's standing in the only open floor space large enough to contain him.

"What's the big deal?" he rumbles at Illian. "The guy's just a target." By his slight smile, I know he's pulling the other man's leg. He knows exactly how hard this is likely to be.

"This man will be surrounded by highly paid and even more highly trained security forces," Illian argues correctly, "on a station that *he* owns and on which seven out of ten people owe their livelihoods to him. Hardly just another target, Mr. Boyd."

Quinn just shrugs. It's Perry who speaks next. "Commander, you seem to speak of this man like you know him. Do you mind sharing with the rest of us just how that might be?"

I hate how perceptive she is sometimes. Like most senior chiefs I've known in the Navy, she issues the question almost as a command, even when directed at a senior officer like myself. I don't take offense—those who do question the wisdom of senior enlisted men and women in a wartime situation—and ours definitely qualifies—don't often live to do so twice, which affords those enlisted salts a measure of respect from any officer worth anything.

Despite all that, I hesitate, worried about how they'll all react to what I'm about to say. But then I mentally square my shoulders—which in real life still sting from Perry's last application of the dreaded burn ointment—and tell them exactly how the man in question knows me and how I know him.

The silence in the room lies heavy after that as they all peer at me in disbelief. For several long moments, none of them speak, though Illian's mouth opens and shuts spasmodically as if he's trying to talk but can't get the words out. Even Perry is speechless for the first time since I've known her. Only Quinn smiles, though this is the part I didn't tell him when we met on the station earlier today.

Finally, Illian finds his voice and breaks the silence. "All due respect, Commander, but let me get this straight. You're telling us that Jackson Hwong, majority shareholder and CEO of Skytran Incorporated and quite possibly the most wealthy and powerful man in the Leeward Republic—possibly in this entire *sector*—is your *father*?"

I nod, trying to meet his gaze levelly but feeling the blood rush to my face and turn it red—well, at least the half of it that isn't a mass of already red and angry scar tissue.

Then I'm gratified to see Illian's mouth drop open again as he shakes his head in disbelief.

"Commander," breaks in Perry, "you may just be the most interesting person I've ever met."

That makes me turn redder, though for different reasons. Then it makes me feel a little sick to my stomach as I contemplate just how much these people *don't* know about me and how their entire attitude toward me would change if they *did* know the entire story.

Because as much as Brad likes to call himself a mass murderer, those five hundred-plus civilians he killed were killed in the line of duty. By taking their lives, he saved ten times as many people on Bellerophon Station. Sure, he doesn't see it that way, but just about everyone else with any sense knows he did the right thing. Even a stodgy group of admirals who, in no real secret, didn't like him much, were realistic enough about the entire affair to issue him a full pardon, though he never did pardon himself.

But as for me, I really *am* a mass murderer. Because my actions at Hothan—telling my dear father where my task force was going to be—killed fifty-seven innocent spacers at Yolandra, and I don't have the excuse of causing those deaths in the line of duty. I killed them because I couldn't say no to my daddy. What a joke. And the thought of seeing Jackson Hwong, who took advantage of me and helped turn me into a traitor and a murderer, makes even my unburned skin crawl and makes me want to go back to my cabin and huddle up on the bed and weep. Seeing him again *once*, two months ago, when he arranged to have his Leeward Republic Navy friends stop and board *Wanderer*, was more than enough for me, but I don't have a choice right now.

To save Brad, I need to confront the man who destroyed my life. And I can't even start to explain to my crew why that terrifies me so much. After all, I let Yancy Jessup, my old captain, do terrible things to me— I can't even say the word in my own mind—all to keep him from telling the world of what Jackson Hwong tricked me into doing.

I feel my eyes start to tear up. Do you know how hard it is to *always* be on edge, to always feel like you're one wrong thought—or one wrong word, or one wrong look—away from breaking down and sobbing? I've felt

46

that way almost continuously for the last four years, ever since the events at Yolandra. In fact, the only times I haven't felt that way lately have been in those few moments when Brad and I have been alone and free to just talk. When I'm with him, it's somehow easier to just be myself—from before *Ordney* and Yolandra—and not dwell on my flaws. Maybe it's because he's so flawed himself, or maybe it's because he's such a goof sometimes that I can't help but feel a little shred of joy in his presence. Or perhaps it's that he's the first person in years who has shown faith in me—not in my rank, but in *me*.

My biggest fear is that, now that he knows my secret, things will be different between us. Assuming, of course, I ever see him again.

*That* lovely thought opens the dam, and tears start to run down my cheeks. They all notice, and the chatter of a few side conversations in the wardroom fades away. I can feel them all staring at me in surprise, which, of course, just makes the tears come faster. What a mess I am.

"We have our orders and our heading," Illian says to the room. "Commander, with your permission, we'll head to the bridge now and get undocked and underway." He doesn't actually wait for my permission for anything but stands and motions for everyone else to do the same. They file out of the hatch after Quinn moves out into the corridor and isn't blocking it anymore. On the way out, though, Illian throws a look at Chief Perry, who sits back down at the wardroom table right next to me.

For what feels like a few long minutes, I do nothing but stare at the table in front of me while tears continue to flow. Perry says nothing, just letting me cry. She waits for me to break the silence.

"You shouldn't follow me, Chief. All of you. I'll just get you killed." The words, so reminiscent of the ones I said to Brad on the first *Persephone*, come out of nowhere but are no less true. Still, Perry's reaction is not what I expect.

"Snap out of it, Commander!" she barks, and I turn in surprise to see a stern look on her face. "Commander Lin, you sell yourself short. I've spoken at length with Petty Officer Harris, and at least half of the daring and genius tactics that you've been so quick to attribute to Captain Mendoza came squarely from *you*. But instead of putting your tactical prowess to work on this all-too-important mission, you seem to be wallowing in self-pity. No officer can afford to put their own feelings in front of her ship or her crew, and you know that. So, I say again, snap out of it!"

I stare at her in shock, my mouth falling open as I struggle to wrap my head around her words. Her mention of Harris also reminds me that I haven't seen much of the man since we got underway in Carter's System, and I wonder what he's been doing. But that thought is only fleeting as I look into Chief Perry's hard gaze. Abruptly, her face softens, but only a little.

"Commander, we've only known you for a week, but simply based on what you did for our system, we'd follow you. Still, you're not going to gain the loyalty you need from this crew until you start acting like you deserve it. You have to stop moping around like a schoolgirl who lost her first love and instead *be* the captain of this ship."

"But I'm not the captain," I protest. "Brad—"

"With all due respect, ma'am. Shut. Up." The words are so jarring that they render me speechless again. This time, Perry doesn't even pause. "I've seen enough of you to know that you were a good officer in the Promethean Navy. Now, I don't know exactly what happened that robbed you of your confidence, but the only one who can fix that is you. And the first thing you need to do is realize that *you* are the captain of this ship, not Brad Mendoza, because he's not here. You are. And regardless of who is in charge after we rescue him, for now, you *are* the captain. Act like it."

Not knowing what else to do or say, I just nod dumbly at her, which seems to at least partially mollify her. She nods back, then stands up and makes her way to the hatch and opens it. But before she leaves the room, she turns back to me.

"Captain, we'll be at Skytran Orbital in about two and a half hours, just in time for the end of their work day. I suggest you use that time to pull yourself together. I will inform Mr. Boyd that he and his team are to be ready to escort you onto the orbital and to your father's office."

I open my mouth to argue—to tell her that I need to do this alone—but the look she shoots me tells me that Quinn Boyd and his five team members will be accompanying me whether I like it or not, so I close my mouth and say nothing.

"And Captain," she continues, "whatever has passed between you and your father, I expect that when you see him, you make him fear you more than he does the fires of Hades itself."

With that, she pulls herself up to full attention and throws me a sharp salute. Then she turns heel and leaves out into the corridor, shutting the hatch behind her and leaving me alone in the wardroom.

# NINE
# NUMBERS

### BRAD MENDOZA

You never realize how wonderful it is to have all ten fingers until you only have nine. That's right, Kayla likes knives. So does Norm—Jerod—and the rest of their merry crew.

This morning, little Kayla cut off my left pinkie when I told her that her black skinsuit makes her look so pale that just being around her gives me all the sunlight I've been missing in this drab little cell.

She didn't like that.

But I think she was more upset that I *still* haven't given them the coordinates of the stellarium deposit. So, she took my little finger and promised to return this afternoon and take…another part of my anatomy, one I've grown quite fond of over the years. Yep, you guessed it, my nose. At least, that's what I'm telling myself she meant.

This is it. I'm done. I've held out for I don't know how long, but I've come to the end.

If this were a story from the *Adventures of Firebrand's Marauders,* I, the hero, would be able to hold out indefinitely under the most severe torture imaginable. In fact, I'd be able to seduce Kayla using my very manly charm and convince her to selflessly sacrifice her life to help me escape. It would be the end of a glorious redemptive arc for her, and I would hold her dying body in my arms as she confesses her love with her last breaths, and then I would yell in manly fashion at the heavens about the injustice of her never having a chance to be with me.

But this isn't a novel, I'm not my hero, Billy Firebrand, and Kayla is a psychopathic sadist who has no redeeming qualities beyond a nice butt. I'm frankly shocked I've been able to hold out this long.

So, when the cell hatch clangs open and Kayla walks in again already carrying her knife—and noticeably wearing blue now instead of black—I'm ready with the coordinates. I expect her to kill me the moment she gets them, part of me is even *hoping* she will, but she's too smart for that. And the threat she levels at me if they prove to be wrong is enough to make me gulp as she triumphantly leaves the room.

## TEN
# STORMING THE GATES

### *JESSICA LIN*

I walk down the lushly appointed corridor briskly, in part because I know that if I slow down now, I might cower from what I need to do next. Forward momentum is about all that's keeping me going at this moment. That and the steady footsteps of the six men and women who surround me, six of the most hardened soldiers I've ever seen, all unarmed—that was my one stipulation to having Quinn and his troops escort me—but looking no less lethal as a result.

Still, it wasn't Quinn or the rest of his intimidating team that got us this far. Rather, it's been a combination of speed and shock that has allowed us to penetrate multiple security cordons and get this deep into the Skytran Orbital executive offices. Speed by never stopping long enough to have anyone properly challenge us, and shock by telling anyone who looked like they might that I am Jackson Hwong's daughter, and they stop me from seeing him at their own peril.

Now, I walk into the man's outer office, flinging the heavy wooden door open—seriously, who puts a heavy wooden door on a space station?—and striding in like I own the place, even though I can feel my legs practically about to give way underneath me.

"Excuse me, you can't be here!" one of the three executive assistants who serve as the gatekeepers to the office almost screeches. I ignore her.

"You best not be getting in the lady's way," I hear Quinn say behind me in his deep baritone voice. "Bad things happen to those who do." Even without a gun, he alone may be the most intimidating man I've ever met, and the five others with us are no slouches either. Brad's going to be happy with the team I've assembled for him, but I push that thought aside. The next few minutes might very well determine if Brad *ever* meets his new crew.

None of the three assistants make another peep as Quinn and the rest glower at them. I haven't even let my steps falter, and I reach the end of the long antechamber and push on the *two* matching doors that appear to be made of the same heavy wood as the previous one.

They won't budge.

I whirl, fighting a wave of rising anger inside, and point directly at the nearest executive assistant, a weaselly-looking man who is practically cowering behind his desk. I know that I'm a sight right now, half my exposed face covered in scars and unhealed burns and the other half set so hard that my jaw hurts from clenching my teeth.

"You," I say simply. "Open it. Now."

The man doesn't even attempt to argue, and a second later, I hear a click as the doors in front of me unlock.

"Boss," Quinn asks casually just before I reach out to push on the doors again, "what do you want us to do if security shows up?"

I turn back and regard him coldly, then point to the assistant who first screamed at us. "Kill her first," I say without a hint of emotion in my tone. But then I give a little shake of my head for only Quinn to see. He nods and winks. Maybe that will keep the inevitable security force out of the office for fear of a hostage situation, but we already set the rules of engagement for this op: no one dies.

Now, I turn back one last time and push the doors open, stepping forward into the extremely large and plush office on the other side. And there, behind the desk a full ten meters into the room, is the man himself: Jackson Hwong, my father.

The last time I saw Jackson was onboard the *Dauntless* when the Leeward Republic battlecruiser waylaid *Wanderer* in this same system. He had me escorted to a conference room, where he spoke sternly down to me about how it was time to stop ruining my life and to 'come home and let him take care of me'. As if he wasn't the one who ruined my life in the first place. That entire conversation, I never said a word but largely stayed curled up in the fetal position in the chair across from him, not meeting his gaze even once.

Now, he's standing behind his desk, a look of pure terror on his face and a pistol in his hand pointed at me but shaking so much I doubt he could hit me if he emptied the entire clip. This time, I don't cower, not because I'm any less intimidated by the man and not because I hate him any more than I did that day on *Dauntless*. No, I find courage this time because *this* isn't about me and him anymore. He had to go and bring my only friend into it.

Without pausing, I stride across the room like I have nothing to lose. Because I really don't.

When I reach the desk, I lift one hand and slap the gun out of his hand so hard that it flies across the room and bounces off the wall. Then I walk around the side of the massive desk to where he's standing, and I strike without warning, my open palm impacting the side of his face in a way calculated to inflict a lot of pain with no real damage. The damage will come later, assuming he doesn't give me what I need.

Any hint of strength or stoicism he may have still had disappears as he cries out in pain, and I don't give him even an instant to recover his wits. I move closer and knee him in the crotch, and as he bends over in agony, I bring my elbow down on the back of his head, hard enough to flatten him to the deck but not enough to knock him out. I need him awake for this next part.

"Jessica, what are you—?" he gasps, but I don't give him time to finish. I wind up and kick him in the kidney with the toe of my combat boot, again, not so hard that it might actually damage anything. Regardless, he screams again, curling into the fetal position on the floor and raising his hands as if to ward off an evil spirit. I haven't even broken a sweat yet, but it's clear my dear father has spent his entire life relying on *others* to do his fighting for him. I wonder if this is the first time he's ever been hit.

"Hi, Dad," I say through clenched teeth. "Miss me?"

He doesn't answer; he's too busy gasping for breath, and this time, I give him the reprieve he needs to recover enough to speak.

"What are you doing?" he says, repeating his unfinished question from before.

"What, not enjoying the family reunion?" I reach down and grab him by the shirt collar and drag him across the floor toward a low, stuffed chair to one side of the room, using both hands now to lift him and practically throw him into it, feeling several new wounds open up on my left side where scabs over barely healed burns break as I flex the muscles underneath.

I can see Jackson is genuinely terrified. His eyes are wide, and he's sweating great drops and shaking so badly I'm surprised he can see me straight. Not that I can blame him for his fear. Anger burns so brightly in me that I can feel it coming through my eyes and directed straight at my father. I loom over him in the chair and give him the hardest glare I've ever given another human being; it makes the glare I once gave Brad for staring at my butt look absolutely tame by comparison. I see him wince, and I know I have him. An odd sense of triumph rises to take its place next to the burning hatred.

"Listen, Dad," I say, spitting out the title like the

swear word it is for me, "I'm going to ask you questions, and you are going to answer truthfully. I'll know if you lie, and I won't need that gun over there to kill you if you do. Got it?"

He looks at me like I'm crazy for a second, searching my face as if to see if I mean it, and I'm surprised to find that I actually do. What he sees obviously convinces him of the same because he nods frantically.

"First question, did you know what Kayla Carter had planned for Brad Mendoza and me?"

By the shocked look on his face—he's well beyond being able to school his facial expressions right now—I have my answer, but I wait for him to say it anyway.

"I...I have no idea what you're talking about."

"Wrong answer," I snarl and slap him hard with the back of my hand, causing him to scream again and reach up with both hands to hold his now-bleeding nose. "Next time," I tell him, "the fist is closed. Want to try that again?"

"Alright! Alright!" he whines, lowering one hand but keeping the other to his nose as if, after everything, he's actually surprised I hit him again. "I knew. But I swear she was only supposed to take your friend, Mendoza, to keep you from galivanting across the galaxy with that—"

As promised, my next blow is with a closed fist and goes right into his stomach, knocking the wind out of him again. He doubles over in the chair, gasping for breath like a fish stuck on dry land. It's with great effort that I don't follow it up with a killing blow to his neck or head, but I stand with my muscles tensed so badly they're shaking as I struggle to bring myself back under control. It would be so easy to…

I give him a slow count of ten to partially recover, though it's really more for me to try and calm myself enough to continue questioning him. Then I reach down and push him back up to face me. "Save your excuses. What was her plan, the rest of it? Where did she take Brad?"

He looks up at me in confusion. "Is that what this is all about? *Him?* He's a disgrace, Jessica, he's—"

The next punch is the most savage yet, and he screams as I break his already-bleeding nose, getting his starched white shirt quite dirty in the process. Again, I resist giving the killing blow, but only just barely. As I watch him weeping now in pain and fear, I feel a rising fear of my own—a small voice that is trying to get me to regain reason—but it's drowned out by the pulsing hate running through me. "Try again, Jackson," I hiss.

"Fine! Fine! She didn't tell me, just that Mendoza had the coordinates of something worth a lot of money, and she promised to cut me in after she delivered you to me unharmed and safe."

"Does this look like I'm unharmed and safe?!" I scream, leaning down so that I'm in his face and pointing to the scarred and disfigured part of mine.

He breaks down now, whimpering, pleading for his life in choking mumbles interspersed with sobs and sputtering. And that's when I see him for the first time, stripped of his station and his money; just a man like any other, one who takes advantage of and hurts people like any other, only with the resources to amplify the damage he does. But now…

I turn and walk across the room and pick up the gun I knocked out of his hand earlier. I stop on the way back to grab a handheld comm off his desk and then I'm in front of him again, the pistol held straight out at his forehead as his wide eyes practically cross to fixate on the business end of the gun.

"Shut up," I command, and he stops his blubbering and begging, something in my voice telling him the alternative is death. "Here's what's going to happen. You're going to call off whatever security team you already have forming up outside, or they'll find nothing in this room but a corpse. Then you and I are going to negotiate the terms of your surrender."

He nods, and I toss him the comm. "On speaker so I can hear it."

My dear old dad does as I told him and calls off his security team. I listen carefully but don't detect anything that sounds like a coded phrase, though I'm sure it would be subtle enough for me to miss it. But I'm also counting on his strong instinct for self-preservation.

When he's done, I put the gun right against his forehead. He starts whimpering softly, and tears fall from his eyes now in great streams down his cheeks.

"Why, Jackson?" There's a pleading tone now in my voice. I wanted to love this man *so much*. "What did Kayla really offer you?"

His already limp shoulders slump even further; there's no resistance left in him. I could ask him for the codes to his blockchain accounts full of billions of credits right now, and he would give them to me without a second thought. "She told me about the stellarium," he whimpers. "She said if I helped her get the coordinates from Mendoza, she'd cut me in. Skytran... our revenues are down. We need the money to meet our debt obligations. Hundreds of thousands of people would be out of jobs. I promise I wouldn't have done it otherwise. You have to believe me!"

I don't believe him, especially the part about him worrying about anyone other than himself, but I also find I really don't care about his motives. "Was Admiral Walters in on it?" I've gone back and forth in my own mind, wondering if the Leeward Republic admiral, who on the surface seemed like a straight-shooter, knew what she was sending us into when she introduced us to Kayla Carter.

"No," he insists. "Not all of it, at least. I asked her for help stopping your ship and then introduced her to Kayla and asked her to hear the woman out and make an introduction to Captain Mendoza, nothing more. She doesn't know about the stellarium. She thought Kayla was actually from Carter's World."

"How were you supposed to get in touch with Kayla afterward?"

"I have no idea where they are! All I have is a comm code and the location of a dead drop on Hope Station. That's all, I swear!"

"Give them to me." I accept a ping from his implant, and he transfers me the code and the dead drop details. From the look in his eyes, he doesn't even consider sending me fake information; he's far too terrified.

"Now," I continue, "let's go back a bit further." This is the hard part—the part I debated skipping but ultimately decided I couldn't. "Did you know, and I mean *know,* what was going to happen at Yolandra after you used me for intel on the *Intrepid* task force's position?" My voice is pleading again. I want him to tell me he didn't know, that he was a pawn like me. Somehow, even after all that's happened, I want to believe he didn't knowingly do those things to me.

But he sinks lower into the seat as if trying to disappear into its plush depths, and I once again have my answer. Four *years* of my life, destroyed because of this man! Four years! And now my naval career over, my best and only friend possibly dead, and nothing in my heart but hatred and grief. All because of him! All because of me and my stupid girlish need to have my daddy. Why? Why couldn't I have just told him to buzz off when he first reached out all those years ago?

My finger tightens on the trigger, coming just to the edge of the pressure required to squeeze it back and have my revenge.

But just as the hate is about to consume me, something else enters my mind:

Power.

The man in front of me, my so-called father, has had all the power over me since the day he first contacted me when I was an eager eighteen-year-old so excited about meeting her dad for the first time. He had power over me when he tricked me into revealing my task force's location at Hothan. And for four years after that, every time I've thought of him—of possibly ever meeting him again—it's sent me into a spiral of fear and depression.

I let two men *rape* me because I was so ashamed of

the power this man held over me and what he had done with that power.

And if I pull the trigger now...I give him all that power back. I'll be letting him once again dictate the course of my life. Because there is one thing I have *never* done. I've never looked a man in the eyes and pulled the trigger that killed him. Traitor and murderer, I may be, but I've never personally fired a weapon in anything other than self-defense. If I do it now when I don't need to, then this man, this worm in front of me, will *always* have power over me because he'll be the one who made me abandon my principles...*again*.

I lower the gun, the hatred fleeing from me as quickly as the gun leaves Jackson's forehead. Part of me expects my knees to buckle now that I'm not sustained by that hatred, but I feel no less sure-footed in this moment than I did a few seconds ago; perhaps I feel even stronger on my feet.

"OK," I say, surprised by the calm in my own voice, "this is what's going to happen next. I'm going to walk out of here, and I'm going to go save my captain. But if the information you gave me isn't rock solid, I'll be back. Understand?"

He nods.

"And just in case you decide to call your security team back and *not* let me out of here, you should know that I've given *all* the information on what happened at Yolandra to an attorney in the Kate's Hope system and another here in Fiori. If I don't check in with them both in the next few days, they'll release the information to the press. And while you may not care about what that will do to *my* reputation, think for a moment what it will do to *yours*. How many companies will do business with a spy? How many customers will trust a man who betrays those closest to him? How many banks outside the republic will simply freeze your assets? Do you understand me?"

He nods vigorously. It's all a bluff, of course. I haven't had time to even talk to one attorney, much less two. And up until this moment, the thing I dreaded *most* in the entire galaxy is exactly what I just threatened. What happened at Yolandra has been my shame for years. I didn't even tell Brad about it until minutes before the explosion that almost took my life. I let terrible things happen to me to keep the secret!

But as I make the threat now, I realize something that I never expected: I mean every word of it. I will burn the universe down around my father without a second thought, even if it destroys what little reputation I still have, if it will save Brad.

That realization floods in and replaces the void left by the hatred I felt for my father. Brad. Even thinking about him fills me with an odd warmth.

The man I leave behind in the office when I turn to go is a whimpering puddle, all power he may have once held over me irrevocably vanquished. But the woman who leaves the office is not the same one who entered. Gone is the hatred; gone is the homicidal rage and the fear of what this man can do to me. In its place is a single thought of Brad and an emotion that I'm not ready to name yet, but that makes me feel simultaneously exuberant at the very thought of him and terrified that I'll be too late to save him. It's all I can do not to run back to my ship and start putting the information Jackson gave me to use.

Nevertheless, I calmly collect Quinn and his team in the outer office, and the three of us walk slowly past a flummoxed and angry security team outside. They follow us back to our ship's docking airlock at a distance but never so much as point a single weapon at us.

Because I have the power now.

As *Persephone* undocks from Skytran Orbital and begins the day-plus journey to Kate's Hope, I find myself feeling pride not in the fact that I could have killed my father with my first blow, but rather from the fact that I did *not* kill him with my last.

Yes, you could say that I'm feeling pretty good about myself, right up to the point when Chief Perry walks onto the bridge and waggles a bottle of foul-smelling lotion at me.

## ELEVEN
# ANOTHER NEW RECRUIT...A WEIRD ONE

### *JESSICA LIN*

A day and a half of transit later and two days on Hope Station, and we have *nothing*. Despite his best efforts, Harris isn't able to trace the comm number we got from my father. And the dead drop location has been a total bust as well. I've had the crew watching it on rotation for our entire time here, and they haven't spotted anyone they think could be part of Kayla's mercenary crew. Of course, my competent crew of spacers isn't exactly a crack intelligence team, and Quinn Boyd and his team stand out even worse than they do. I find myself desperately wishing I'd taken more naval intelligence training back in my Academy days, but there's little I can do about my lack of expertise now.

It's been a month since Kayla took Brad, and I feel no closer to finding him than I did the first time I woke up in the hospital on Carter's World.

Remembering how he and I found Owen Thompson's target on the Rishi Paradise almost two months ago, I've been spending a lot of my time in station bars, listening and fishing for information. But unlike Rishi, I don't find the info in the first, second, or even third bar I visit. In fact, two days and seven bars in, I have exactly *nothing* to show for my efforts.

Which has me seriously contemplating the untouched glass of scotch in front of me in the seventh bar. It's a dim and dingy place, the kind that makes your skin crawl at the thought of what it would look like with the lights turned up. The floor is sticky, and the place smells of cheap booze and sweat, which makes me oddly melancholy—it reminds me of Brad's quarters before I managed to dump all of *Wanderer's* supply of alcohol down the galley sink.

I've tried everything in the hour that I've been here. First, I chatted up the bartender, but whenever he wasn't fixating on my scars, he was staring at my chest. I wonder what he would think if he knew the scars extended down there as well.

Next, I tried a few of the bar's patrons, but they either ignored me or tried to convince me to go with them back to their ship or to a rent-by-the-hour station motel. One even tried to put his hand on my inner thigh. Not wanting to draw too much attention, I bent his finger far enough back to make him flee but not quite enough to break it.

After all that, I've given up. So now I'm in a booth in

the back, contemplating my next move and finding I have zero ideas as well as zero intel. The heady rush I felt four days ago in Fiori when I extracted the information from Jackson Hwong has faded entirely, and I feel like I'm back at square one.

Just as I'm about to either knock back the scotch or get up and leave, a woman I've never seen before slides uninvited into the booth across from me.

"Hola, princesa," she says before I can demand an explanation. "Couldn't help but notice you over here all alone. I'm called Uvalde. You?"

I frown and study the intruder. She's shorter than me with dark olive skin and sharp, though not entirely unattractive, features. But her two loudest characteristics are her spiky neon blue hair and the large silver nose ring that looks practically white against her complexion.

"Not to be rude," I tell her, "but I'm not interested in…companionship right now."

She laughs out loud. "Ah, princesa, no offense, but you're not my type. I prefer the hombres. Besides, I think you are here looking for something else I *can* give you."

I contemplate this for a moment. I was about to leave anyway, but it's not like I have anywhere else more productive to be. Talking to this crazy woman might at least be a distraction for a few minutes.

"And just what is it you think I'm here looking for?"

She grins. "You're here because you need to hire me, princesa."

I can't help but snort a laugh, though her continuously calling me 'princesa' is already wearing thin. "Oh, really. And what makes you think that?"

She shrugs, the grin still plastered on her face. "Because you're looking for information, and I'm the kind of chica who can get you any information you need."

"I highly doubt that," I reply, shaking my head in the recesses of my hood.

"Tell you what, princesa," she says, leaning across the table, "if I can tell you all about yourself, when we two have never met, then hear me out. I get anything wrong, I leave. Deal?"

Intrigued despite myself, I nod.

"Perfecto. OK, listen. You're obviously ex-Navy. The way you sit—it's a dead giveaway."

I raise my eyebrows. "And what makes you think I'm not still in the Navy?"

"Simple. Those scars I can make out under your hood, princesa. The Navy would have fixed those up. But you're still walking around with them. That and no self-respecting officer would be caught dead in a place like this. And you were an officer by the way you carry yourself and talk. Promethean if I got the accent right, and from the clase alta out there. Probably went to some fancy private school. Verdad?"

I try hard not to show my surprise at how accurate her guesses are thus far.

"But you've fallen on hard times," she continues with a shrug. "Happens to the best of us. So, you're not here on behalf of your Navy, which means you're here for something personal. Which means you're looking for something or somebody. But you gave up after less than an hour here, which isn't surprising, princesa. You are *so* out of place in this bar."

She pauses, eyeing me with a small grin.

"Wait," I ask, "you've been watching me this whole time?"

Her grin widens. "Sure, princesa. What, thinking you would have noticed an amazingly guapa señorita like me watching you for the last hour? Well, let's just say I'm good at not being noticed when I don't want to be, entiendes?"

I shake my head in genuine awe. "OK, I'll admit, you've got me pegged pretty well. But that still doesn't tell me why I should hire you."

She shrugs and then suddenly reaches out and grabs the drink from in front of me, knocking it back in one shot before I can protest. She grimaces and wipes her mouth with the back of her sleeve as she sets the glass down.

"Gross, princesa. I hate scotch. You trying to poison me?"

OK, I was certainly right about this woman being a good way to break up the monotony of the evening for me, but now I need to extricate myself from whatever this is. She's definitely got a screw loose. An excuse to leave is forming on my lips, but she speaks before I can get it out, leaning forward and eyeing me with a serious expression for the first time.

"Listen, princesa. If you really want to find the hombre you're looking for and whoever took him from you, then having a bunch of space cadets who look way too much like cops watching a dead drop is a sure way to warn whoever you're after that you're coming. But give me twenty-four hours, and I will find your hombre for you. De acuerdo?"

My mouth drops open in surprise. It's always a little funny when Brad does it, and I guess I picked up the habit from him.

"Bueno," she says without waiting for me to verbally agree. "I'll meet you at your ship tomorrow. But until then, you pull those space cadets back, and you stop going to bars and looking all conspicuous and obvious like. You'll just get in my way."

All I can do is nod dumbly, not even stopping to think how she already knows what ship is mine or the fact that we haven't even discussed her pay rate.

## TWELVE
# WELL, WELL, WELL. IF IT ISN'T THE CONSEQUENCES OF MY OWN ACTIONS

### *BRAD MENDOZA*

I estimate it takes Kayla about five days to check on the coordinates I gave her. That tells me something; it means that we're almost certainly only a single jump point away from Gerson. There's little chance she could have sent a ship, checked the coordinates, and gotten the ship's return message in that little time if we were any further away.

That narrows our location down to about a dozen systems, though if I assume that she's not dumb enough to hide inside the Promethean Federation, then that really only leaves four systems, of which only two have inhabited worlds, and I would think she'd want to be somewhere where she can get supplies.

Great. I've narrowed down my location to just two

systems. That would be wonderful if I could do *anything* with that knowledge.

Or if I wasn't very likely about to have one of my favorite appendages cut off.

Kayla storms into the room, and I've never seen her this mad. Her face is tight with anger, and her lips are curled into a snarl that reminds me of a cougar that once took one of my grandpa's cows on the farm. Except there's no grandpa here with a bolt-action rifle to take the cougar out.

Just me and my nine fingers.

"Brad, do you think I'm *playing* with you?!" she practically screams as she pulls to a stop in front of where I'm huddled on the hard metal deck. For once in my life, I keep my mouth shut and don't answer with some flippant remark calculated to send her even more over the edge.

"What did you think giving me some random wrong coordinates would accomplish?" she says, spittle flying as she leans down and yells in my face. "I'm going to make you regret screwing with me. I'm going to hurt you so badly you'll beg for death before you give me the *real* location of the stellarium!"

That commences a truly inspiring meeting of Kayla's steel-toed combat boots with my head, shoulders, knees, and toes. By the end, I'm worried I might have brain damage, and I can barely breathe through all the cracked ribs. I finally get to learn what the term 'sobbing mass' means because that's exactly what I am now.

She finally relents and storms out of the room, screaming all sorts of threats and invectives my way, including a few words that would make even my old foul-mouthed subordinate, Ensign Stevens, blush.

I spit out a tooth—not as fun as it sounds—and allow myself a small measure of hope. Because despite what Kayla may think, the coordinates I gave her were *not* random. When I last saw Agent of the King's Cross Heather Kilgore on that little asteroid in the Fiori system, I asked her for two things: first, the signed-over title and registration for the *Wanderer*; and second, for a way to send a distress signal to her if the worst should happen. In response, she gave me a set of fake coordinates in Gerson to send anyone who tried to get the real ones out of me.

Assuming Kilgore is anywhere near the Gerson system, Kayla just unknowingly tripped the ultimate trap because now the King's Cross agent knows I've been taken. And as good as Kayla is, she's got nothing on the King's Cross. I might even allow myself to feel a little bad for her when Heather Kilgore comes calling.

No, I won't.

## THIRTEEN
# WHAT HARRIS HAS BEEN UP TO

*JESSICA LIN*

To my utter and happy bewilderment, it only took *eighteen* hours for Hayley Uvalde to find the next clue to Brad's whereabouts. And she does it in the most obvious way possible, which has me wanting to slap myself in the face for not thinking about it myself.

She *calls* the comm code Jackson gave me. After a few minutes of pretending to be his personal assistant, she gleans enough from the man on the other end—despite his multiple protests and demands to speak to Jackson directly—to have a very solid idea of where we need to go next.

So now, the next evening after our meeting in that bar, a widely grinning Hayley Uvalde is lounging in the captain's chair when Commander Illian and I walk onto the bridge to start the undocking procedure. She's just sitting there, one leg draped lazily over the arm of the chair, noisily eating an apple. Her hair is green now.

"What's up, boss?" she asks around a mouthful. Next to me, Illian stiffens. From the first moment he met her, Uvalde has rubbed him the wrong way. He's only known her for half a day, and already he dislikes her.

"Get out of the chair, Uvalde," I say in a longsuffering tone. I'm doing it mostly for Illian, who might have a brain aneurysm if I don't kick the green-haired woman out; in reality, I'd let her sit in that chair all she wants if she can lead us to Brad.

Uvalde hops out of the chair instantly and throws a wide grin at Illian, making his mouth tighten into a hard line. "Hey, Illy," she says, and the nickname turns that stern look on his face into a frown. Uvalde pretends not to notice and instead sits down on the hard deck next to the chair, crossing her legs and continuing to munch on her apple. I walk gingerly around her and sit in the chair she vacated.

"Captain," Chief Perry's voice interrupts. I turn to see my self-proclaimed steward and motivational speaker looking at Uvalde with a bemused expression. Then she looks up at me. "Mr. Harris has requested that you meet him in your cabin as soon as we undock."

I feel my face redden and look around at the rest of the bridge crew, expecting to see embarrassed glances my way. Because even though I know that Harris isn't inviting me to my own cabin for…well, for *that* reason, it can only sound that way to the rest of the crew.

None of them seem to even notice. Though Perry is

wearing an odd smile that makes me think she knows what the meeting is about, which puts her one up on me. I've been intending to visit Harris at some point today anyway to find out just what he's been up to in his quarters the past week and a half, but I guess I'm about to find out.

"Very well," I say. Then I set about getting us undocked. When that's done, I give Illian the conn and excuse myself to go find out just what is going on with our resident makeup artist and tech guru.

Despite Perry's lecture to me about being the ship's captain, even temporarily, I've never actually used the captain's quarters on *Persephone*. Instead, I've set myself up in the XO's quarters, leaving Brad's room vacant and open for if—no, *when*—we rescue him.

But I arrive at my quarters now to find them empty. Sighing and cursing Harris' absent-mindedness, I walk the few short steps down the corridor to the captain's cabin, open the hatch, and step inside…

…to find myself in a forest of people.

That's the best way I can think of to describe it. Because there are about five people taking up the very small space of the cabin's outer office, except that four of those people are fake. Harris stands in the center of the others, beaming proudly while surrounded by what looks to be four blow-up manikins wearing a variety of very green clothing, hence the impression of a forest.

"Jessica," he says excitedly, "what do you think?" He raises his arms and motions to encompass his four blowup friends. For my part, I don't answer, still a little too stunned at what I've found here.

His grin falters, but only for a second. Then he

moves to one of the manikins, which is wearing a long flowing dress that looks like it's made from forest green silk. "This one is my favorite," he says without further preamble. "The green will bring out your eyes so much better than that horrid red dress you wore on the Rishi Paradise. And notice how it lays across the shoulders."

Stunned, I stare at the dress, then at him, and then back at the dress. I barely register the comment about the dress I wore on the Rishi, except to think that I remember it looking really *good* on me. And by the way Brad couldn't stop staring at me while I wore it, I think he agreed.

"Harris, what are you doing?" I ask finally.

His smile disappears, and he looks confused. "Giving you the new wardrobe I made you, of course," he says as if it's the most obvious thing in the world.

I sigh. "And *why* do I need a new wardrobe?"

Now, he looks at the plain blue skinsuit I've been wearing during most of my time on *Persephone* as if the answer to that question should also be obvious. Then he shrugs. "I just figured that with your...you know," he motions toward the scarred side of my body, "that you'd want something to wear that's more comfortable *and* a little more stylish."

I immediately start to bristle at the reference to my disfigurement but stop myself. Harris, for all his awkwardness, is probably the most earnest person I've ever met, and I have to remind myself that he views another person's appearance in the same clinical way that Brad and I view a tactical plot. There's no judgment in his eye beyond that of a professional looking to help his subject. I just really don't want that subject to be me right now.

Though…

I step over to one of the manikins that's the furthest from the entry hatch and regard it. Harris moves up next to me and looks over his creation with me.

"It's Aurellian leather," he says excitedly.

"Where did you get the funds for Aurellian leather?" I ask, dreading the answer. Maybe the ship's account has even less money than I thought.

Harris only shrugs. "I have money. I mean, Owen used to pay me enough, and I never really had much to spend it on, so I used some of it for this."

Taken aback, I realize with a start that *we* have still never paid Harris anything. I say as much now.

He shrugs again. "I figure you and the Captain are good for it. Just pay me whenever you can."

Strange man.

I turn my attention back to the equally strange yet oddly compelling outfit on the manikin in front of me. As Harris said, the entire outfit is Aurellian leather, which, when I reach out to feel it, is so soft and supple that it reminds me more of silk than leather. Except it also feels sturdy and resilient.

It's green, just like the dress and the other two outfits I haven't examined yet. And it covers the manikin's entire body save the hands, the head, and one shoulder. I notice with appreciation that the uncovered shoulder would be on my unscarred side, whereas on the left, where my scars are, the outfit covers all the way up to the neck and has an attached hood that I could pull over to shroud my face.

"It's two pieces," he explains excitedly. "And both the pants and the top have zippers up the sides that allow you to get in and out of it easily. You know, for when you have to put on that really bad-smelling lotion."

I turn and regard him again. I *knew* the lotion smelled a bit odd, but I'd convinced myself that no one else noticed or that the smell faded enough after I put it on. Apparently not. Leave it to Harris to make such a clinical observation and give me a complex for the rest of our voyage. But I shake it off as best I can and nod appreciatively. The outfit *does* look easier to get out of, even compared to my skinsuit.

"I also think it looks kind of intimidating," he says now with a wry smile. "Like a warrior goddess would wear it while vanquishing a monster of some kind."

I shake my head and try not to laugh. Who knew that Harris could wax poetic? But apparently, we're in his world now, and I can add fashion designer and tailor to his strange and eclectic list of skills and expertise.

"Can I?" I ask, and he immediately takes the outfit off the manikin and hands it to me.

I excuse myself and go into the empty bedroom, closing the hatch behind me. There, my back to the full-length mirror, I change into the new outfit. After a brief hesitation, I decide to rip the band-aid off and turn to regard myself in the mirror all at once.

I'm almost stunned by what I see. With the way Harris designed the outfit, and with my short black hair hanging forward across the left side of my face as I've taken to wearing it, I can almost imagine that half my body *isn't* covered in scars. Just like the traditional ship-board skinsuit, this outfit also hugs the body, but the thicker leather makes it feel like it covers me so much better, and I can't make out the texture of the scars beneath it at all like I can with the skinsuit. I immediately feel less self-conscious about them. Sure, during an explosive decompression, I'll miss the skinsuit, but otherwise, I like everything about the new outfit.

But perhaps the most stunning part of the transformation is the way it changes my *overall* look. For the past four years, ever since the events at Yolandra, every time I've looked in the mirror, I've seen someone ranging between a semi-competent naval officer and an incompetent traitor. What I see now is so wildly different. The outfit has an old-fashioned look to it that I would almost call medieval, and the first word that comes to mind when I see it on me is 'mercenary'.

I move my hair out of my face tentatively, and what I see now sends a shudder through me. Combined with the archaic look of the green and black leather outfit, the scars covering the left side of my face give me a hardened look. And for a brief moment, the abject fear I saw in my father's face when I burst into his office makes sense. Because I don't look like a timid naval officer anymore. I look like someone with death on their mind. I look pissed off, which fits because I most decidedly am.

Turning slightly to examine the back, I give an approving nod, then blush involuntarily. I'm not sure I can *ever* wear this around Brad once we find him.

Because it hugs my curves better even than my skinsuit, and he'll *never* be able to stop looking at my butt. The thought makes me laugh a little to myself, though even a couple of months ago it would have—it *did*—enraged me. I'm not sure what that means, though there's something about it that makes me smile a little.

Regardless, when I finally step out of the small bedroom and back into the office area where Harris waits, I brace myself for his usually critical eye to point out all the flaws in my appearance, but I'm surprised when he just stops and stares at me, mouth agape.

"Jessica," he says, and then he abruptly stiffens his posture and throws me what for him would count as a sharp salute. "I mean, Commander Lin, you look… awesome."

Despite myself, I smile, ruining the effect. "I love the outfit, Harris. Can you make a few more just like it?"

He considers this and then nods slowly. "I don't have enough Aurellian leather for more than two at the most, but I can mix in some other fabrics and make it work. I bet when Kayla and her crew see you coming, they'll wonder if Hades itself coughed you up to go after them."

That makes me blush again, at least on the undamaged side of my face. But then I feel myself flush with a different emotion because, while Harris means well, he just verbalized what I've been worried about this entire time: my scars have ruined any beauty I may have once had. Now, I'm a pale apparition of what Jessica Lin used to be. That shouldn't matter to me; I've spent *years* convincing myself my looks are more of a curse than a blessing, but they're still a part of me, I suppose.

Nevertheless, I reflect, turning and catching my reflection in the office's smaller bulkhead-mounted mirror. At least Harris is right on one thing: Kayla and her mercenaries are going to learn to fear me before this is all over.

## FOURTEEN
# THE KING'S CROSS IN PERIL

### *BRAD MENDOZA*

 The torture Kayla subjects me to in the half day or so after she learns the coordinates are fake is some of the worst I've ever experienced. Luckily, she doesn't cut off my nose—or any other favorite appendages—but she does just about every other horrible thing to me that I can imagine. Despite all that, I'm able to hold out because I now have the greatest weapon a prisoner can have: hope.

As I endure the most horrific tortures that Kayla and her sick little friends can devise, or as I lay bleeding and broken on the hard metal deck, waiting in dread for the next session, I listen for the sound I hope to soon hear: gunshots and screaming men and women as the fury of the King's Cross descends upon them in all its murderous glory.

Unfortunately, when it does come, it's not with a bang but with a whimper.

The hatch to my cell clangs open, and a man I've never seen before enters. He's tall but has a belly that makes him seem almost as wide, and his face wears the most ridiculous mustache I've ever seen. He obsessively and absent-mindedly twists one end of it with his hand while he stands gazing down at the mass of skin and bones that *used* to be a Promethean Navy officer. I'm pretty sure I don't even look human at this point.

"So, this is the little scum who killed my brother?" the man growls, almost to himself.

Then he kicks me...hard. I'm sorry, no offense to Kayla, but her kicks just don't hit the same, no matter how well placed, as a kick from a big man like this. His shoe hits me solidly in the stomach, and I vomit, gratified that a decent amount of my meager stomach contents now reside on the man's shoes.

He swears loudly, and Kayla steps inside the room and surveys the scene. I see her smirk behind the man's back but then wipe the grin from her face as the guy turns around and looks at her.

"Why is he still alive?" he demands.

"Well," she says coolly, "he's alive because I still need him alive."

The answer doesn't satisfy the man with the stupid mustache, and he waves one beefy hand my way. "The Hades spawn should have been dead *weeks* ago. You telling me this little weasel has held out on you this long? What are you doing, tickling him until he gives you the coordinates?"

If I still had the capacity to laugh, the image of Jerod or one of Kayla's other minions tickling me would make me do so now. Instead, I curl up into a tighter ball and try to make myself so small they'll forget I'm here.

"Listen, Poulter," Kayla says in a hard voice, and the name immediately gets my attention. I brave another look at the large man, and now I can see the family resemblance to the pirate captain we took down in Carter's System. All the way down to the penchant for stupid black leather.

"You don't get to give the orders here," Kayla continues. "He will stay alive until we don't need him anymore. Period."

The guy seems like he's going to argue again but catches himself at the last second and shrugs instead. "Well, hopefully, the new little present I brought you will help with that. Who knows, maybe *she'll* have the coordinates if Mendoza doesn't."

My heart, which already isn't in a good place, sinks so low I think it might squeeze out from the bottom of my feet.

Sure enough, another burly-looking guy—pirate by the way he also thinks studded black leather is a good look—enters the room, shoving a lithe red-haired woman in front of him. She's black and blue all over, and it looks like she's endured a pretty bad beating herself. Her lip is fat, her nose crooked, and both her eyes are black; one of them swollen shut.

Heather Kilgore, intrepid Agent of the King's Cross, has finally arrived.

The man shoves her to the floor next to me, and she falls with a dull thud and a groan.

Poulter sneers, as does Kayla, and then they turn and leave the room, the other pirate trailing behind them. Someone closes the hatch, so I lift my head and look over at my new cellmate.

"Welcome to Chez Kayla," I say in what I intend to be an ironically cheerful voice, but it comes out more like the croak of a frog followed by a coughing fit as my bruised stomach revolts. I throw up again. Lovely.

Kilgore frowns at me but says nothing.

"You know," I say after wiping my mouth as best I can on my shoulder—my hands are still tied behind me, "when I sent my captors to those coordinates you gave me, I was *expecting* you to follow them and *rescue* me, not join me in my cell."

She grimaces. "You're telling me. This wasn't exactly the plan. But there was a pirate ship waiting at the jump point exit when I followed them through from Gerson. It was on me before I could even make a run for it. I'm not a naval officer, after all. I usually shoot at people face-to-face."

"Well, there's always room to learn," I say. "So, what now? And by the way, we should probably assume they're listening to everything we say in here."

She throws me a look that tells me I'm stating the obvious. "Well, my original plan was to storm the place and take care of you. Now, we'll have to improvise."

"Oh sure... Wait. 'Take care of me'? You mean, like *kill* me?"

She shakes her head in exasperation. "Come on Mendoza. What did you *think* was going to happen when you got captured with those coordinates rattling around in your head?"

"Well," I admit, "I kind of thought you were going to *rescue* me!" I yell the last part, or at least try to. It comes out more like the rasp of a dying horse.

She scoffs. "Not even *you* can be that naïve."

I am, but now she's hurt my feelings, so I'm not going to admit to it.

She starts to move across the floor toward me, a little like a worm since she's also bound hand and foot, and I do my best to scramble away.

"Mendoza, stop it!" she snaps. "I'm not going to kill you now. That just leaves *me* here for them to interrogate. I just want to talk more privately."

I consider kicking her and trying to caterpillar my own way to the other side of the room, but I relent and stay put while she worms her way to where our heads are almost touching.

"Does Commander Lin know where you are?" she asks in a whisper.

It's like someone rips a bloody bandage off and pours rubbing alcohol all over an open wound, and I can't find the air to answer her for a few seconds. When I do, I can barely get the words out. "Jessica's dead. They blew up her ship." I've managed to largely *not* think about that since being imprisoned. Every time I do, it makes my insides hurt worse than anything Kayla has done to my outsides. But the deep anger and hatred I feel toward my captors over their murder of Lin has been the single largest motivator to *not* give them anything.

Silence. Then, a sigh. "Sorry, Captain. I imagine you

two had grown close. And that means we'll have to figure out our *own* way out of here."

I frown at that. "You mean the rest of the King's Cross doesn't know you're here?"

Another pause. "They would if any of them had been in Gerson with me. But since you left the Federation, a few other brush fires have sprung up that have required our attention."

I don't find myself caring enough about my old star nation to dig into that. When I don't respond, she continues.

"I have to admit, I'm impressed you've held out this long. From the looks of things, you've been here a *while*. Maybe you're not the weak man your superiors thought you were after Bellerophon. But now we both have to turn our attention to escape because *no one* is coming for us.

Great. Maybe I should just call Kayla back here and let her kill me now.

# FIFTEEN
# UNEXPECTED GUESTS

### *JESSICA LIN*

The reaction I get when I first enter the bridge in my new mercenary outfit, just before we get to our jump point, is just as terrifying and exhilarating as I expected. Illian watches me in utter shock, Perry smiles and nods her approval, and the other officers and enlisted spacers show various reactions in between. For someone who has tried very hard and mostly unsuccessfully for the last four years *not* to be the center of attention, it's nerve-racking but also somehow gratifying to be so now.

It may sound childish, mostly because it is, but when I sit down in the captain's chair again, dressed like this, I don't find myself automatically going with the ramrod straight back and posture of a naval officer.

Instead, I find myself almost lounging in the chair, as if the new clothes have suddenly imparted an entirely different attitude into me. And maybe they have. I just don't know yet if that's a good or bad thing. All I know is that if Brad could see me now, he'd…well, he'd probably say something inappropriate and obnoxious that would ruin the moment, but he'd be drooling all over himself while he said it. Is it weird I *miss* the guy so much?

The spell is broken when Hayley Uvalde wanders onto the bridge and takes me in with one astonished glance. Good to know someone is going to fill in for Brad in that department.

"Whoa, princesa guerrera!" she exclaims. "You know how I said I prefer the hombres, boss? Well, you might be changing my mind."

Suddenly extremely self-conscious, I blush and sit up in my chair, returning to my customary straight-backed posture. "They're just clothes, Hayley," I tell her, "Harris made them because they'll be easier to work with when I have to get my daily treatments."

She grins, not buying my excuse. "Sure, those are just clothes like body armor is just a bike helmet. They may serve the same purpose, but they are *not* equal. Anyway, my name's not Hayley today; it's Sabrina."

I eye her skeptically, forgetting for a moment my own embarrassment. "What do you mean, today it's Sabrina?"

"Names are like clothes," she winks at me, "you can change 'em whenever you want, princesa. I decided when I got up this morning I didn't like Hayley anymore, so now I'm Sabrina. Simple."

"Uh, Uvalde," I say uncertainly, "that's not how names work."

"Sure it is," she says with an even wider grin like she's the only one in on some cosmic joke, "you change your clothes so you can go all princesa guerrera; I change my name so I can feel more like a Sabrina today. Everyone needs to feel like a Sabrina every once in a while. No es asi?"

I just shake my head at her but choose not to disagree further. I'm quickly learning that arguing with Uvalde is a great way to get a migraine.

We finally reach the jump point, and it's a long one. The next ten hours pass in almost agonizingly slow fashion as we fly through the strange gray of jump space toward the Capaldi system, where Hayley— Sabrina—Uvalde's trail of breadcrumbs is leading us. Capaldi is in the direction of Gerson—just one jump away from it—as I suspected, but it's not one of the systems Brad and I passed through on our circuitous route to Kate's Hope when we were first fleeing from the Promethean Federation.

I am gratified, and actually quite surprised, that even four weeks after leaving Carter's World, the 'temporary' repairs President Carter's people did to *Persephone* are holding up incredibly well, with no signs of leakage or hull degradation, even at the weld points. Still, I know we'll need to be careful about presenting our starboard side to any enemies we might run across; the hull there is still significantly weaker than on our undamaged port side.

"Unidentified ship approaching at oh fourteen mark two relative," Illian reports crisply just minutes after we exit jump space. "They are not running a transponder."

"I see," I say, pulling up the sensor readout on my implant, which shows nothing more than a yellow dot, signifying a contact of unknown intent, burning toward us almost head-on. "Let's not take any chances," I tell him. "Make sure all missile tubes are loaded and charge the laser capacitors. We'll be ready if they're hostile."

The sinking feeling in my stomach tells me that they almost certainly *will* be hostile. Even if they simply weren't receiving our hails, interstellar navigational laws specify that the ship leaving a jump point has the right of way. To still be burning toward us on a direct intercept course and not giving way means that the captain on the other ship is willfully ignoring those laws. Add to that the fact that his acceleration is far above that of most civilian crafts, and it's almost certainly a warship or warship analog streaking toward us.

And they're already in weapons range.

"They're hailing us!" Robinson calls from the sensor and comm station. "Recorded video message."

"On screen," I tell her.

The image of a mustachioed man in all black leather appears on Persephone's forward viewscreen as Lieutenant Robinson puts the message up for all to see. The guy is sitting on the bridge of what looks like a similar class ship to our new *Persephone*. He's actually twisting the end of one side of his ample mustache, making him look like a cartoon villain and even drawing a guffaw from *Sabrina* Uvalde from her customary place on the hard deck next to my chair.

"*Corsair*," the man starts, using the name of our ship from when Poulter and his goons still owned it and making my stomach sink even further, "this is *Hawk-wing*, Captain Lawrence Poulter in command." That does it; my stomach now may as well be in my feet. "You stand accused of murdering my brother and stealing that ship from him. Surrender your captain to me for trial and execution and surrender your ship, and I will allow you to cram into a single escape pod and launch yourselves toward Christos. You have two minutes to signal your intention to comply with my generous offer, or I'll blow you out of the sky."

The recording cuts and I look around at my bridge crew. "Observations? Options?" I ask them, my voice surprisingly calm for all the somersaults my stomach is doing.

Illian speaks first, as I would expect from a tactical officer. "Scans show a frigate analog out-massing us by about twenty-five percent. She's been heavily modified, but the ship catalog suggests she's an older Koratan design, similar to *Persephone*. It's hard to tell from here, but it looks like they've welded on some additional laser projectors, and I'm seeing something that looks like a ship-killer-sized missile tube retrofitted in their nose. If I had to guess, I would think it's a one-shot weapon; no way they're carrying more than a couple ship-killers on that thing."

I nod my agreement, even though *one* ship-killer is still terrible news. That and the ship's greater mass, along with our already damaged starboard side, means that we will be heavily disadvantaged in any engagement.

"Commander," Lieutenant Robinson pipes in, "we have the acceleration edge on them by about four percent, but at this angle of attack, there's no way we can run from them. They'd be on us before we could change vectors sufficiently to avoid them." Just as I thought.

"I recommend we increase acceleration to full military power," Illian suggests, "and try to shorten the engagement envelope as much as we can, and then hit them with everything we have in passing." There's a hint of excitement in his tone. None of us have any doubt that the pirate captain is indeed the brother of the Poulter who held Carter's System hostage. And since Kayla killed *that* Poulter, with Brad's help and mine, this may be the closest my new crew can get to taking revenge.

Still, Illian's excitement doesn't make his suggestion wrong. It's standard tactical doctrine for an engagement like this. Except that, for all the reasons I already named, it's also the *wrong* move. We simply cannot rely on the chance nature of a head-to-head battle. In fact, even if we survived it, all *Hawkwing* would have to do is execute a turnover and fire that ship-killer right up our exhaust flare as we pass. And a missile, even a large one like a ship-killer, can accelerate a *lot* faster than any warship. After all, it doesn't have to worry about converting any people inside of it into so much gooey paste if the g-forces bleed through the compensators. Bottom line, we *have* to try something that doesn't involve a stand-up shooting match.

My brain kicks into a strange sort of high gear, a state that I've been able to achieve sporadically since my screwup on *Ordney*, but that used to be the norm for me in high-pressure situations like this. As it thankfully does so, I consider and discard a dozen options and finally arrive at the one with the highest likelihood of success. Except my crew definitely won't like it.

"Lieutenant Robinson," I bark. "Signal back to the *Hawkwing*. Tell them we are willing to negotiate the terms of surrender."

As one, every face on the bridge turns to regard me in shocked silence. Robinson makes no move to follow the order, instead staring at me with her mouth open in surprise.

"Follow the order, Lieutenant," I tell her calmly. "I have a plan."

Just not a good one.

## SIXTEEN
# A RECKONING

*JESSICA LIN*

Quinn Boyd is *not* a happy man. Though I hired him as a shooter for the eventual liberation of our captain, he's quickly come to see himself as my personal bodyguard. His loyalty and concern are more appreciated than I can even express to him, but in this regard, right now, I'm going to piss him off.

"Quinn," I tell him—I still haven't figured out what, if any, rank to give him as a member of our little crew, so we all just call him by his first name, and he doesn't seem to mind, "you *can't* come with me. One look at you, and those pirates will know I'm up to something."

I can tell by the expression on his face that he sees the logic in that but that he's just spitting mad enough to ignore it. And if this man, who leads the only six fighters on my crew, decides to disobey my direct order, I'm reasonably sure there's literally nothing I can do about it. I'm not even paying him enough to threaten to take *that* away.

"You're not going over there alone," he says sternly, and I open my mouth to argue, but he cuts me off before I can start. "Heddy is going with you. End of discussion." He says it with such a finality that it shuts me right up, and I look over at Quinn's informal second-in-command, Heddy Rodriguez, a trim and tough-looking woman only slightly taller than me but built like a whip. She's standing at Quinn's side, and her glare is almost as severe as his, like she's daring me to disagree with her boss.

My shoulders slump. "Fine, but we'll both have to be unarmed."

Heddy shrugs. "No matter. I know six different ways to kill a man with my little finger."

I snort a laugh, but by the looks on her face and Quinn's, it probably wasn't a joke. "Fine," I say again and turn back to Quinn. "You good on your part of the plan?"

Now, the big black man smiles, though it's a smile that reminds me of a moray eel as a fish swims in front of its den. "Sure, Boss," he rumbles. "Let's just hope the guy buys your bluff."

I nod, not willing to tell him at this point that I'm *not* actually planning to bluff Poulter. It's better he doesn't know that part, though I feel terrible for Heddy, who will be putting her life on the line along with mine. For a second, I almost tell them both the full extent of what I'm planning to do, but I stop myself. I can't risk the big man telling me flat out I can't go. If he does, *all* of us are dead.

"Well, let's be on with it then," I say as gruffly as I can manage with a lump in my throat and turn to walk toward the airlock, the undamaged port airlock, which is now securely docked with the slightly larger but much better-armed pirate vessel *Hawkwing*.

Heddy steps up beside me and keeps pace. Unexpectedly, as soon as we're out of hearing range of Quinn, and just as my conscience is about to get the better of me and warn her anyway—no matter the consequences—she speaks.

"Boss, you're planning something *really* stupid, aren't you?" she asks with a smirk.

It's actually the first time we've spoken alone since she came on board just six days ago with Quinn. I've gotten to know a few of Quinn's shooters, and he introduced them all to me when they first arrived on *Persephone*, but Heddy has been the most silent of the bunch, preferring to stay in the background despite how much Quinn obviously relies on her.

"What makes you think that?" I ask cautiously.

"I seen the look in your eye," she answers frankly. "Last time I saw that was in a man who was about to go on a suicide mission and had made his peace with it."

I grunt. "It's not too late to turn back, you know. You can tell Quinn I ordered you to leave me or that I hit you."

She laughs lightly, though I'm almost sure I could take her in a fight if I got the drop on her. Marines like her are tough and wily fighters, but I'd wager I'm better without a weapon just like she's no doubt far better *with* one.

"Boss," she says, "I like you. I like your style. And I think that you and I will be walking back on board this ship alive. Until then, it's my job to keep you that way."

I sigh as we reach the inner airlock door. "Fine, but don't say you weren't warned."

There's no time to say anything else as we quickly cycle through the airlock and find ourselves facing two large men in studded black leather head-to-toe. One of them confronts each of us, signaling for us to raise our arms so they can check us for weapons.

What follows is a very humiliating and *extremely* thorough pat down. The guy in front of me now knows my butt better than Brad does. I hear a grunt to the side and look with horror to see that Heddy has kneed her guy right in the crotch, causing him to remove his hands from her chest and instead use them to cradle his manhood. As he sinks to the deck in pain, I brace myself, but his buddy only laughs hysterically and grabs me and then Heddy each by an arm, leading us further into the ship while the guy Heddy kicked hobbles along after us.

Five minutes or so later, we enter the warship's bridge to find Lawrence Poulter sitting on an abnormally raised captain's chair that reminds me of a throne from an old movie. He's still twisting one side of his mustache as he was doing when he first called us. He regards me coldly as I enter, his eyes only momentarily twitching to take in Heddy before he stares back at me, looking me up and down and licking his lips.

Pig. His gaze sends an involuntary shudder through

me, and I'm suddenly very grateful to Harris for putting me in a thicker material than a skinsuit. I'm wearing my 'princesa guerrera', or 'warrior princess' outfit, as Uvalde calls it—unfortunately, the rest of the crew has already started calling it that as well.

Poulter's eyes stop on the scars covering the left side of my face. "I hope my brother did that to you," he says with a sneer.

"Nope," I say in as flippant a voice as I can muster. "The woman who killed your brother did this to me after she put a bullet through his chest. Maybe you know her. Little thing, mean temper, goes by Kayla." It's true, though he immediately looks dubious.

"Look," I say, not wanting to let him think too hard about things, "we're on our way to kill her right now. So, if you're really that set on getting revenge for your brother's death, you'll let us go so we can get it for you."

He laughs, a great booming sound that temporarily throws me off. Not that I actually expected him to bite on that, but he doesn't even stop to consider it.

"No, no, no. I have a better idea," he says. "We're going to take your ship, then you're going to tell us everything you know about my brother's death. Then we'll kill you and whatever sad little crew you have with you."

I guess his promise to let the rest of the crew cram into an escape pod launched toward Christos, Capaldi's one inhabited planet, is no longer on the table now that he actually has me in his clutches.

At least he's only threatening to *kill* me. There's not even a single mention of him having his way with me first. Maybe he's a progressive pirate. Or maybe he thinks that's already implied. Or maybe he just doesn't like my scars. Either way, I hope I won't have to find out.

I shrug, really going for a nonchalant look as if I don't care what he does, doing my best to channel Brad but probably failing miserably. Really, I'm just playing for time, and I'm extremely happy when my implant suddenly pings me. It's Quinn telling me he's done his part, and we're ready to roll the dice.

"Listen, I know you think you're in control here," I say, again doing my best to sound unconcerned, though my voice rises a bit higher than I would like, belying just how nervous I really am. "But truth is, I hold all the cards."

He grins, twirling his mustache again. "Oh yeah, and what's a pretty piece of flesh like you know about cards?"

There it is! I knew he was a misogynist at heart, not the progressive pirate after all.

I shrug again. "I know that I'm the one whose crew just planted sixty pounds of C8 spread across various points on your outer hull, all controlled by a deadman's switch in my implant. If my heart rate spikes above one-eighty or below sixty, boom, your ship is gone." I reach up and snap my fingers to punctuate my threat.

For several seconds, no one speaks, and then Poulter lets loose another hearty laugh. He clearly isn't taking me seriously, so I do the one thing I promised—or at least heavily assured—Quinn I wouldn't. I pull up a menu on my implant and select one of the ten explosives at random, praying that Quinn and his men are where they're supposed to be: far enough away and back inside *Persephone* through the emergency dorsal hatch.

The deck beneath me shakes violently, and a few of the pirates fall to the floor. I keep my footing but wince. That was a little *too* close for comfort. Maybe I should have double-checked the explosive's location before I remote detonated it.

"Sir," screams a man at one of the bridge stations. "Decks three and four are open to space on the port side!"

"You—" Poulter screams, calling me a name that no woman should ever be called. I force a tight smile in reply despite every centimeter of me practically trembling with fear and adrenaline.

"Board their ship and kill every single person aboard!" he growls next, but before the pirate he points at can leave the bridge to carry out his orders, I trigger another bomb, this one more carefully chosen, and the bridge shakes again though the explosion sounds farther away.

"Stop!" the pirate captain yells, and all movement on the bridge comes to a screeching halt, every eye riveted on me.

"I'll make it stop, Poulter," I say, putting all the hard edge I can into my voice. "But not until I'm back on my ship and out of range. Then you'll be able to go out and take the bombs off your hull without them auto-detonating."

He glares at me, and if looks could kill, I'd be dead a dozen times over. Slowly, finally, he nods. "Fine." But by the fire in his eyes, I know this isn't over.

Still, I don't plan to give him time to reconsider or do anything drastic, and I motion at an amused-looking Heddy to follow me as we depart from the bridge, retracing steps by memory until we arrive back at the airlock and are relatively safe onboard *Persephone*.

Quinn is waiting for us when we enter through the inner airlock hatch. And by the look on his face, he is *not* happy. "You!" he booms, leveling a finger at me as soon as I'm on board. "You're insane!"

I meet his gaze impassively and just nod. "Get used to it." Then I push past him and make my way briskly to the bridge before he can see just how badly I'm shaking.

My reception on the bridge is a bit better, with most of the crew staring at me in awe, though both Illian and Perry frown but say nothing.

"Chief," I say to Jensen, "get us undocked and out of here, full military power."

"Can't, ma'am," he says dejectedly. "They still have the docking grapples into us."

"Open a channel," I order, and then I say loud enough for the bridge speakers to catch my voice, "Poulter, release the grapples now." I punctuate my demand by exploding another of the bombs Quinn and his team affixed to their hull.

"It's done, you psycho—" I cut the line before he can call me a name again and glance over at Jensen. He nods to indicate the pirates have retracted the grapples.

"Full power, now," I tell him calmly, and I sit in my chair just as I feel *Persephone* surge beneath me, the compensators struggling to keep up with our breakneck acceleration. Without being asked, Illian throws up an image from a rear-facing camera on the main viewscreen, and I can just make out the pirate ship tumbling away as our drive exhaust hits it. I smile.

"That won't stop them," Quinn rumbles, and I look up in surprise to see he followed me onto the bridge. "If anything, they'll be even more intent on taking us out now. You should have stuck with bluffing like we discussed."

I shake my head. "Mr. Boyd, demolitions and ordnance may be your area of specialty, but I used to be in the Promethean Navy. Pirates are *my* area of expertise, and there's only one way to deal with them: explosively."

He doesn't laugh at my lame attempt at a joke. Brad would have somehow landed that one. I shrug it off. "Besides, this way, at least they're damaged, and we stand a better chance in a fight."

Quinn grunts noncommittally and fixes his gaze on the forward viewscreen where Illian has replaced the image of the quickly receding *Hawkwing* with a sensor plot showing us rapidly widening the gap.

"You know," the big man says, "it will only take them a little while to get out there and find the remaining bombs on their hull and disarm them."

This time, he's absolutely right, and I nod. "Then we just need to hope it takes them long enough for us to build up a good lead."

It doesn't, and even with our faster acceleration, we're still within weapons range when the *Hawkwing* pivots in space to fix the giant borehole of its ship-killer missile tube right on our retreating exhaust plume.

## SEVENTEEN
# DEATH MOVES QUICKLY

*JESSICA LIN*

Until today, I've never been on board a ship that had a genuine ship-killer fired at it. Oh sure, when we'd fight pirates in the Federation, they would occasionally decide to fight back instead of just running away. But none of them had more than simple ship-to-ship medium missiles if even that. A ship-killer is an entirely different thing, and they're mostly only carried by station defense platforms and capital ships.

First of all, and maybe counterintuitively, the bigger the missile, the faster it goes. A big missile like a ship-killer has plenty of room for multi-stage booster rockets and the fuel it needs to reach an absolutely unfathomable level of acceleration.

Let me tell you, the simulations don't do that acceleration justice. Maybe that's because even in the most realistic simulation, you *know* that the missile hurtling toward you is just a bunch of qubits in an AI program. But now, with a genuine nuclear-tipped ship-killer bearing down on me, the little blip that represents that giant missile is moving so quickly across the sensor plot that I feel like I barely have time to think before it will close the distance to our fleeing ship.

"Launching countermeasures!" cries Illian from the tactical station, thankfully doing his job without waiting for specific orders. That snaps me out of my own shock, and I start shouting orders to the rest of the crew.

"Jensen, cut acceleration and pivot us to present our port broadside," I order my helmsman. "Perry, launch a full spread of ship-to-ship aimed at *Hawkwing* as soon as we're oriented correctly." The older woman nods from her place at the auxiliary weapons console and does as commanded. I want to give Poulter something to think about in case he magically has another ship-killer to load in that massive missile tube, but I don't want to distract Illian from playing defense against the missile already en route.

"Interceptors away," he says, his voice now calmer than before as he launches a spread of smaller anti-missile ordnance, nicknamed interceptors in most navies and apparently also in Carter's World's system patrol. A set of four smaller blips join the six medium-sized ones Perry launched racing away from our ship in the general direction of both the *Hawkwing* and the incoming ship-killer.

We watch with bated breath as those dots all start to near each other. First, the six ship-to-ship missiles we launched cross paths with Poulter's ship-killer, but neither reacts to the other. Then, the four interceptors close with the larger missile, and the five points all converge. I can't breathe, can't even think, as I wait for Illian to call out the results.

"Misses, all of them," he says somberly. "Launching another spread." Four more interceptors appear on the plot, but I know as well as he does that if the first four missed, the next set, with even less time to steer toward the oncoming missile, aren't likely to stop it.

"Laser defenses!" I cry out. "Local control!" With that order, the eight port laser clusters start to spear the space around us with their deadly beams of light. Each laser has its own rudimentary AI controller, with dedicated bandwidth and a direct feed from the ship's sensors. They track the missile and fire faster than any human could do in their place, and the silence of their firing, even inside the ship, is eerie as the sensor plot updates to show lines representing their beams.

As the missile nears, two circles appear around the dot representing *Persephone* on the sensor plot. One is yellow, and the large missile crosses inside that perimeter even as it appears. The other, inside the first, is red. An explosion inside the yellow may cause light damage. Inside the red…they'd be lucky to find enough atoms to determine what happened here.

I'm holding my breath again, feeling that unique blend of responsibility and utter helplessness that has plagued ship commanders since the beginning of time. Whatever happens next is on me, but I have to trust my crew and the ship's AIs to do their jobs without my interference. Even yelling out orders now would do nothing but distract them all.

Then, just as the massive missile is about to cross over the line of the red circle, Illian whoops in triumph, and the dot representing the ship-killer winks out as one of our laser banks finds its mark.

"Brace!" is all I have time to yell before *Persephone* starts to spin wildly, and I black out from the sudden g-forces as our ship tumbles through space, propelled by the blast wave of the devastatingly large nuclear warhead that detonated as soon as the little AI brain in the ship-killer knew it was doomed.

My vision clears a few painful seconds later as *Persephone's* primary AI responds and fires the thrusters to bring us back under some semblance of control. I had it easy, I realize, as I look to see Haley—Sabrina?—Uvalde picking herself up from the deck where she's fallen in a jumble with Quinn Boyd against the rear bulkhead. Luckily, and by some miracle, neither of them looks seriously hurt. The rest of the bridge crew was strapped in, though a few still look groggy.

"Report!" I call out to no one in particular.

"Damage reports coming in," Perry calls from her station. "Nothing severe yet. Just a few broken bones and a minor leak in engineering."

I nod in relieved acknowledgement.

"Ship-to-ship missiles are reaching the enemy now," Illian says in a voice that sounds half drunk.

I turn my attention back to the plot in time to see two of the three remaining missiles we launched—*Hawkwing* must have taken out the other three—miss the enemy ship by sizeable margins. But then the third and final missile slams into the pirate, and I watch in satisfaction as the sensor plot shows a simulated explosion against the enemy's starboard hull.

I smile tightly. Even a small blast like that should... The plot suddenly shows three more explosions from the pirate ship.

"Those fools," breathes Quinn just loud enough for me to hear, "they didn't disable the bombs on the hull. The impact must have triggered them."

Before I can respond, another massive explosion appears on the plot, and when it clears, *Hawkwing* is nowhere to be seen.

"Their reactor blew," Illian reports, his voice as disbelieving as Quinn's a second ago. Complete silence descends across the bridge. Because while those men and women onboard *Hawkwing* were our enemies and would have destroyed us without a regret, the thoughts of the fiery deaths they all suffered violently and suddenly are sobering. I imagine that's even more so for my crew members from Carter's World—this is likely the first time they've fired, much less killed in anger.

Me? I'm already a mass murderer, just like Brad, but it still shocks me to the core.

It's both a triumphant and reflective crew that starts to burn away from the scene of the battle an hour later after we repair the worst of our luckily very light damage.

# EIGHTEEN
# SERIOUSLY, NAZIS IN SPACE?

### BRAD MENDOZA

 "**I** know what happened to Jessica on *Ordney*," I say conversationally. Heather Kilgore has been largely silent since our first conversation yesterday—I think—when she was deposited in the cell with me. We've tried to whisper to each other a few times to brainstorm plans of escape, but we have fewer options available to us than I had trying to take out that Koratan destroyer with my old ship, *Persephone*.

Regardless, she looks up at me now with her eyebrows raised. This should be a relatively safe topic, even with Kayla and crew listening in, so long as we avoid specific details.

"She told you." It's a statement, not a question, but I nod anyway. "Then you better understand what happened on *Persephone* as well. You understand *why* it happened?" This one *is* a question.

I shrug, as much as I can lying on the hard metal deck with my arms tied behind me. I shove down the horrible grief I still feel anytime I think about Jess—I'm the one who *started* this conversation, after all; no use breaking down in tears over it. That wetness on my face is just my eyes watering from allergies.

"Not really," I admit. "Sure, she made a mistake on *Ordney*, but I just don't get how that made her *let* those terrible things happen to her." I'm telling the truth; it's been bugging me since…well, since Jess died, in the few very dark moments I've allowed myself to think about it.

Kilgore frowns at me, flipping her head a little to get a sweaty string of red hair out of her face. "Seriously? Come on, Captain. You, of all people, should understand what a single bad decision can do to a person's head. Look at how you turned out after Bellerophon. Needless to say, you haven't exactly morphed into a pillar of mental health or self-confidence."

"No," I shake my head, ignoring her amateur psychological assessment of me, even if it is right. "The situations are different. Jessica made a mistake, but it was just that, a *mistake*. And she made it with good intentions, not understanding the consequences. My decision *wasn't* a mistake; it was intentional, and I made it knowing that I was probably going to regret it."

To my surprise, the red-headed assassin laughs, which quickly turns into a choking cough. I wait for her to finish, and when she does, she looks me dead in the eye with her one eye that isn't swollen shut. When she speaks, her voice is harsh.

"You know, Captain, I'm as familiar with your record as anyone who didn't serve with you can be— even the classified parts. Despite the way you talk about yourself, you're *not* an idiot. In fact, the only real sin you ever committed was to think outside the neat little box the admiralty drew around you and every other officer. They hated you for it, but even the ones who hated you the most always had to admit that you were *good* at your job, even if you were an annoying little jerk about it."

"Uh, thanks?" I say, confused.

"Which is why I find it hard to understand why you can be so incredibly *dense* about your former XO," she snaps. "Jessica Lin, Brad, was a perfectionist. Every-thing about her upbringing, her naval career, *everything*, was founded on the principle that she could somehow be *perfect*. That made a big mistake like the one she made at Hothan and Yolandra loom even bigger in her mind, not because she *knew* the consequences ahead of time, but because she *didn't*. So, she almost certainly spent nearly every waking minute since then and up until her death questioning her own judgment and asking herself over and over again what she missed that would have told her that her dear father was playing her."

She pauses, and when she speaks again her voice is more subdued.

"You ask how she let those men rape her to keep her secret? I ask how she could even function on a daily basis with that much self-doubt and self-recrimination always in the forefront of her mind. Keeping her in the Navy was the *worst* thing we could have done to her after her screwup, because she didn't feel worthy of staying. And having others find out about her sin—about how unworthy she really was, at least in her own mind—*that* was a nightmare she wasn't even willing to contemplate."

She stops, turning away, clearly signaling that she's said all she intends to on the matter, and I consider her words carefully. Was Jessica's passivity toward her assaulters just another form of self-punishment like my drinking after Bellerophon? Or like the way I pushed my wife, Carla, away, no longer thinking I deserved her, and right into the arms of another man? It's amazing how self-reflective you get when you're being tortured to death over several weeks.

Suddenly, the anger I've felt inside since learning what Jacobs and Jessup did to Lin on *Persephone* boils to the surface again, far stronger than before. Those men not only took advantage of her body, but they took gross advantage of her broken mind, and at least one of them, Jessup, knew exactly what he was doing when he threatened to reveal her secret publicly if she didn't go along.

If either of them were in the room with us right now, I'd find a way, restraints and all, to choke the life out of them. I feel a burning need to escape so I can *find* them and do just that.

"You get it now," Kilgore says softly, and I look up to find her watching me again. I just nod in reply, not trusting my voice.

We're interrupted by the sound of the cell hatch

opening. I look up to see Kayla enter, this time in company with another man I've never seen before. But it's not a pirate this time, and the sight of the newcomer makes every muscle in my body clench.

The Nazis are here.

There's a section on Earth's Second World War and the Holocaust at the Promethean Naval Academy. It's part of an advanced ethics class for officers and is meant to teach us what happens when military officers follow orders blindly. It's the one and only nod in our academy days to the fact that sometimes it's morally right to *refuse* an order; the rest of the classes focus on *following* orders, which I was never all that good at.

As I've said before, we didn't spend much time studying star nations that Prometheus didn't consider a threat. But we did spend some time on the Jutzen Collective because *everyone* in the Fringe considers them a threat.

I've never understood how the citizens of entire planets can be swayed to follow the orders of the men—only men, never women—who have ruled the Collective as iron-fisted Fuhrers since its formation four hundred years ago out of the ashes of the Polemic Civil War. But one of those citizens now stands before me, though I don't think I'll get the chance to ask him how he sleeps at night, nor do I suspect I would like his answer.

He wears an all-black uniform with red trim. On his shoulder is a bright red swastika behind the image of a ship-killer missile. Taken together with the double pips on one side of his high black collar, it's the unmistakable uniform of a commander in the Kriegsweltraum-marine, the Jutzen Navy.

"This is the one?" the man asks in a cold voice and in a very fake-sounding German accent, stepping over to where I'm lying on the floor and looking down at me with an almost clinical air of detachment. It makes me shudder involuntarily. Look up evil Nazi soldier in the dictionary, and there's undoubtedly a picture of this guy.

Then I notice the double lightning bolts on the other side of his collar and feel the blood drain from my face even more. This isn't just a Jutzen officer; he's a fanatic, a member of the dreaded SS, the Schutzstaffel, the Fuhrer's most dedicated—and insane—followers. These guys make what I did at Bellerophon look like a trip to the store on a Sunday. They would have steered that doomed refugee ship into Bellerophon station just for laughs.

"Yes. And he's close to giving us the information your Fuhrer wants," Kayla says, somewhat lamely as if she's already said as much to the man a few times before but is still afraid of how he'll respond.

He says something back, but I'm not paying attention because my stomach just clenched in the same way it might if I were hurled off a tall building to my death.

Kayla's mysterious employers are the Jutzens?

My mind immediately envisions the Fringe overrun by a navy of unstoppable Nazi warships with stellarium hulls, impervious to most weaponry and crewed by brainwashed fanatics for whom the lives of others are just obstacles to be overcome on their way to building their Fuhrer's glory.

The thought makes me wretch, and my only regret is that my stomach is empty, so I can't vomit on *this* guy's shoes. How are there still people in this galaxy who look at the atrocities of a man like Adolf Hitler and think, 'Hey, that was a great idea; we should do that again!'? It sickens me to the core.

"You have two more days," the SS officer says to Kayla in the same voice he might use when commenting on the weather. "After that, we take him aboard *Brandenburg* and interrogate him properly. And the woman, whoever she is."

Kayla says nothing but seems to shrink and just nods. It's incredible how quickly she's gone from a confident, psychotic, mercenary leader to a timid underling in the presence of this man. It's hard to blame her; the SS are the stuff nightmares are made of.

The man turns heel and stalks out of the room, but just before he exits the hatch, he turns back and tosses something at Kayla. She's taken by surprise and fumbles the item and then drops it, bending over to pick it up quickly from the deck before I can entirely make out what it is. The SS officer frowns as he watches her, as if her inability to catch it has somehow confirmed his already low opinion of her.

"Use that if you must, Fraulein," he says coldly, and then he's gone.

Kayla quickly follows him out of the room, shutting and locking the hatch behind her.

Next to me, I hear Kilgore groan.

"What?" I ask her. "What did he give her?"

"I'm only guessing, but ever heard of truth serum?"

I crunch up my face in confusion and then wince as I

shift my weight, and every beaten muscle in my body complains. "I thought that was just a myth. I mean, I know there are chemicals that can loosen the tongue, but our military implants counteract those automatically, don't they? Don't they?"

"They do," she says, "for the known ones. But word is, the Jutzens have developed something new. I guess we'll find out together if that's true."

Wonderful. Because even if I would be OK with Kayla learning the real coordinates to the stellarium, just to make all this end, there's no way I can let the Jutzens know. Because then the blasted Fringe-forsaken *Nazis* would be unstoppable! And even with me and Jessica both dead and gone, my *mother* still lives in this galaxy.

# NINETEEN
# CONFESSION

*JESSICA LIN*

Running into Poulter and his crew in the outer system reinforces that Capaldi is the place where Kayla is holding Brad. And the irony of the late and unlamented Lawrence Poulter clearly working for the woman who *really* killed his brother is not lost on me.

Still, even with that tacit confirmation, I feel like we're still incredibly far away from finding our captain. Because space, even inside a single system, is *huge*.

Seriously, the entire reason why Kayla and others seem so intent on getting the coordinates in Gerson that Brad may or may not actually have in his head is the same reason why we now stand very little chance of actually finding him in time to stop them. It can take months, even on a fast warship, to search an entire

125

system—years if you need to search the surface of every planet, moon, and asteroid. And every second it takes us to do so is one more second that Brad might break, give Kayla what she wants, and get himself killed... assuming that hasn't already happened.

But instead of being out on the bridge leading the charge in that desperate search, I'm here, in my day cabin, huddled on the couch in the fetal position and shaking uncontrollably, my skin still stinging from the latest of Perry's near-sadistic lotion applications.

I'm not stupid. I know that Brad thinks I'm some sort of tactical genius. And I'll admit, I do have my moments, like just now in defeating *Hawkwing*.

What Brad doesn't know is that the first time I felt that way since Yolandra was when he pushed me to come up with the plan to destroy the Koratan enemy ship in Gerson, back on the first *Persephone*. But despite these recent flashes of my old self, I'm still the same broken woman I was when Brad first met me—who let terrible things happen to me after I killed dozens of people through my own stupidity and weakness.

Brad didn't see me in that escape pod after he stayed behind on *Persephone* to blow it up and take out the Koratan destroyer. I was a wreck. Poor Petra Yesayan and Peter Stevens spent hours trying unsuccessfully to calm me down as my mind spiraled through all the various self-recriminations for getting Brad killed because I couldn't come up with a better plan. The only thing that pulled me out of *that* spiral was when we detected Brad's escape pod and learned he was still alive.

I'm spiraling in equal fashion now, even though our

engagement with *Hawkwing* was, by any measure, incredibly successful. Even so, this time my brain is torturing itself with all the ways things *could* have gone wrong in that fight. And from there, I'm spiraling into all the thoughts of how unlikely it is that we'll actually find Brad in this system, much less alive. But, unlike back at Gerson, Brad isn't waiting just a few kilometers away in an escape pod to help me calm down.

The hatch out into the corridor opens, and a slight figure fills the doorway. I see through my tears that it's Harris. I want to tell him to go away, to leave me alone, but I can't form the words or get enough air to speak.

Silently, he shuts the hatch behind him and moves over to sit on the floor next to the couch I lie on and says nothing, giving me unwanted but much needed company, without judgment and without price.

This isn't the first time he's done this. Brad will never know, but the night I caught Kayla and him kissing on the farmhouse porch on Carter's World, I came back to the *Wanderer* and cried for hours, though even now, I can't say why. Harris must have heard me that night through the bulkheads because he overrode the lock on the hatch to my quarters and did the same thing: he just sat down next to me and gave me silent company. At first, it really creeped me out, but after a while, it was oddly comforting. That's also when he told me I remind him of his little sister, long dead in an accident he refuses to say more about.

Five minutes pass before he finally speaks. "It worked, Jess. It worked. Everyone is OK. I mean, Quinn might kill you next time he sees you, but everyone is OK."

I try to laugh through the tears, to assure him I'm also OK, but I can't even muster the lie.

"I know you're worried about finding the Captain," he says. "But he's a wily guy. If anyone can survive this long, it's him. My guess is that he's just sitting there insulting them and making them question their life choices."

This time a laugh does escape my lips because I can picture Brad doing just that.

"See, he'll be fine," Harris soothes. "And he'll probably ask us what took us so long as soon as we rescue him."

I can feel my body starting to calm as he talks, his voice and his assurances slowly pulling me out of my doom spiral. Finally, I catch enough breath to speak. "Harris, I... Brad... He and I... I..." I can't get the words out, can't even fathom why I'm *trying* to get the words out, to admit something to him that I haven't even been able to admit to myself.

He hushes me. "I know, Jess. I know. And the Captain loves you, too. He'd be insane not to."

The floodgates open again, but this time, the tears have a cleansing quality as I finally face the thought that's been hovering at the edges of my mind ever since that overjoyed moment more than two months ago when I realized that Brad was alive in that escape pod. It pulled me out of my spiral then. And it's part of what stopped me from killing my father back on Skytran Orbital, and I haven't even been able to name it in my own head.

But now I do. I love Brad Mendoza. Assuming he's still alive. He'd better be!

Harris stays with me until I finally fall asleep; when I wake up, he's gone, but a new warrior princess outfit, made with the same Aurelian leather as the first, though this time in red, is laid out carefully on my day cabin desk.

# TWENTY

# THE BEEHIVE

## BRAD MENDOZA

Something has Kayla and her crew in a tizzy. The Nazi must have left a few hours ago, but for about the last hour, I've heard footsteps running or walking faster than normal in the corridor outside our cell. Kilgore and I have listened to voices yelling out there as well, though they're far too muffled to make out what they're saying.

"Be ready," she whispers. "Whatever this is, it may be the only chance we've got."

Great. Even if I wasn't tied up right now, I'm pretty sure at least half of my bones are broken, and I *know* I'm malnourished. About all I *can* do is vomit on any of Kayla's crew if they get too close to me. I'm good at that.

But Kilgore is right. Whatever's happening out there is a deviation from the norm, and that means someone might make a mistake. And if they do, we need to be ready because...Nazis.

# TWENTY-ONE

# THE NEEDLE IN A HAYSTACK

*JESSICA LIN*

"Boss," give me half a day alone on station, and I'll find your novio," Uvalde says—I think she's going by Katrina today; apparently, Sabrina didn't match her mood when she woke up—as she leans back and puts her feet up on my day cabin desk. At least she mostly calls me 'boss' now instead of 'princesa'.

"Capaldi Station has a certain reputation," Quinn Boyd rumbles from his standing position next to her. "You shouldn't go alone. Let me go with you or send one of my people. Heddy could blend in with you. Just two girls out on the town."

"No way," Uvalde answers. At least her last name never changes. "Heddy looks at every man like she wants to kill and eat him. No subtlety at all with that mujer. And you, cabrón, you're too big. They'll take one look at you and pee themselves."

"Katrina," I say, gratified to see from the way she perks up that I've properly remembered her latest first name, "Quinn's right; you should take *someone* with you. If for no other reason than to report back if you get in trouble or need more time. Otherwise, we'll have to send in the cavalry even if you're just running a little late. And that would be *really* conspicuous."

She considers this for a moment, and I get the distinct impression that she's somehow chewing on my words to see how they taste. I'm not sure where that mental image came from but spending even a few minutes with Uvalde can twist a person's mind into a pretzel.

"Claro," she finally concedes, "but I can't take Quinn or Heddy. They scream soldier. I'll take this chico instead."

We all look where she's pointing, and despite all of us no doubt looking confused, no one looks more bewildered than the man she's pointing *at*, Commander Illian.

"Me?" he says in something halfway between a question and a gulp.

"De cierto," Uvalde confirms. "You look Navy, but maybe you can look like a Navy chico on liberty with a pretty señorita, sabes?"

It takes a few moments for the implications of her statement to sink in, but when they do, Illian blushes a deep red. I just shake my head.

"Fine, then," I say, desperately wanting this conversation to end before Illian has an aneurysm...or my headache gets any worse. "It's settled. Commander Illian goes with Uvalde."

"Come on, Loredo," Uvalde says, standing up. "Let's go."

"But my name is Francis!" Illian protests while also rising from the table.

Uvalde frowns. "Not today, Illy. An hombre named Francis is way too buttoned up for a mission like this. But an hombre named Loredo, well, he's got a certain…"

Blessedly, whatever Uvalde is saying fades from my hearing as she and her latest victim head down the corridor toward the airlock.

"Chief," I say next, turning to Perry, "any thoughts on getting us any new missiles to replace the ones we fired?"

Perry frowns. "Capaldi may be an independent system with a questionable legal system, but you still can't just go and buy ship-to-ship missiles on the station's main concourse. I'll ask around as much as I can without drawing too much attention, but my guess is we're out of luck. They don't even have a system defense fleet here; they rely way too much on their supposed neutrality and the fact that they're close enough to both the Republic and the Private for either to take too kindly to someone else moving in and taking over."

I nod morosely. It's about what I expected. I turn to Quinn next.

"You and your team have everything you need?"

It's his turn to frown, but I'm pretty sure that's because he's still mad at me for the crazy stunt with the bombs on *Hawkwing*. "We've got about as many guns and bullets as my shooters can carry. Wish I had a bit more C8 leftover," his frown deepens in my direction, "but what we have should be sufficient if it comes down to that."

I feel a grateful sigh escape my lips involuntarily. It's nice to hear at least *one* thing that's going right for us today.

But my relief is short-lived because, at that moment, Lieutenant Robinson's breathless voice comes in over the intercom. "Commander, you'd better get up to the bridge!"

"What is it, Lieutenant?" I ask.

"We've got company. Looks like the Collective is here."

## TWENTY-TWO
# JACKBOOTED THUGS

### *JESSICA LIN*

A groan escapes my lips despite my best efforts as I stand next to my command chair and look at the image that Robinson has thrown up on the forward viewscreen.

Just as she said, the Jutzen Collective is here, and they're here in grand measure. Coming around the curvature of the planet Christos and aimed directly at the orbital station where we're docked is a behemoth of a ship bristling with enough weaponry to destroy *Persephone*, Capaldi Station, and even the few urban centers on the planet below us.

A battleship. The only thing worse would be a fleet carrier full of fighters.

"Ma'am," Robinson says, "we're being hailed."

"On speakers," I order, and the next voice I hear somehow reminds me of a snake covered in castor oil.

"*MV Persephone*, this is *SMS Brandenburg* of the Fuhrer's Kriegsweltraummarine. Vizeadmiral Heinrich requests the pleasure of your commander's company for dinner this evening. We can see the damage to your starboard airlock, so we will send a shuttle to station docking bay C32 in one hour. You may bring two escorts. Glory to the Fuhrer. *Brandenburg* ends transmission."

With that, the line cuts without even waiting for a response. The message is clear: they know that with that ship in orbit, there isn't anyone within two jumps with the firepower to tell them no…to anything.

"I don't like it, Commander," Quinn rumbles from beside me.

"I don't either," I admit. "But I also don't see that we have much choice. Did you notice how they mentioned seeing the damage to our starboard airlock? What may sound like a simple observation was likely a not-so-subtle reminder that they're already close enough to see *and* target any part of our ship. If we so much as release our docking clamps or bring our reactor to power, they'll know about it."

"So, what are we going to do?"

I consider that for a moment, thinking through the various angles and evaluating options. In the end, I essentially have none. Even if we could run, I need to buy time for Uvalde and Illian to find out exactly where Brad is.

"I suppose I get dressed for dinner."

Somehow, despite being absent from the bridge

when *Brandenburg's* call came through, Harris is waiting for me outside my quarters when I arrive to get changed and cleaned up for my unwanted dinner appointment. As soon as I open the door, he ushers me inside and makes it immediately clear that I will have *no* choice in how I prepare for my visit to the Jutzen battleship.

Thirty minutes later, I emerge from my quarters wearing another green outfit—this one cut more like a Navy uniform, complete with a full commander's rank insignia—my hair done up and makeup on the undamaged half of my face that, to me looks almost cartoonish but that, according to Harris, represents the latest style in the Jutzen Collective.

Wonderful. At least I might impress the Nazis before they kill us all.

My mood is grim as I meet Quinn and one of his men—Paul is the second biggest shooter behind his boss—at the airlock. To my surprise, they're both wearing versions of the same uniform I am, only in shades of red. They even have rank insignias: Quinn's are those of a Marine major, while Paul's are those of a gunnery sergeant. I give Harris, who's followed me to the airlock, an appraising look. He's been busy.

"Commander," Quinn greets me with a nod, all business, but he throws a grin toward Harris. "We're ready to escort you to the shuttle. But I want to make one thing clear. We *stay* with you. If they try to turn us away at the shuttle, you're not getting on board. If they try to make us stay on the shuttle once we dock on that behemoth, you're not getting off the shuttle either. Clear?"

I nod, equal parts annoyed and touched by his dogged determination to keep me safe. "That's fine, Major," I say, nodding toward the rank insignia on his shoulder, "but understand that I may not be able to take you with me into the actual dinner with the admiral on that ship. And I'd appreciate it if you don't start a war we can't win."

He frowns but nods sullenly. Then we're off.

We make our way through the port airlock onto the station and then up two levels to the C gates. When we arrive at gate C32, ten minutes early, there are already two junior officers there in Jutzen Collective Navy uniforms, black with red trim and knee-high boots that frankly look equal parts intimidating and ridiculous.

One of them steps forward as we approach. "Lieutenant Commander Lin," he says, showing that they know exactly who I am—like Brad, I'm getting the impression that *everyone* in the galaxy not only knows we're still alive, but also what we're up to at all times, not that I've made any particular effort to hide it lately. "I am Leutnant zur See Klein, and it is my honor to escort you this evening."

The words are friendly, though the hard look on his face belies any thought that this is simply a social visit. And the glance he throws at Quinn is like that of a man suddenly sucking on a very sour lemon, reminding me that, even with all courtesies in place, this man is still a Nazi.

I take a moment to suck a deep breath and let it out slowly, doing my best to calm my already-frazzled nerves. When I respond to Klein, I'm actually proud of how steady I sound.

"Thank you, Lieutenant *Junior* Grade. Shall we get underway?" I'm gratified to see him frown at my emphasis on 'junior'.

But he nods and clicks his ridiculous heels together and then turns and enters the station's docking airlock. Quinn follows before I can, and Paul takes up a rear-guard position, though he's trailed by the other, as-of-yet-unnamed Jutzen officer. Five minutes later, the shuttle undocks and begins a slow journey to the waiting battleship, which has taken up an orbital position a mere twenty kilometers from the station.

Luckily, when we arrive in the massive battleship's shuttle bay and finish docking, Klein and the other officer make no attempt to make my escorts stay behind. Instead, all three of us are escorted through the expansive corridors of the kilometer-long warship. In fact, I have the distinct impression that we're being led the *long* way to wherever it is we're going, and that the ship's commander has made a point of having almost every one of the vessel's two thousand crew and officers stationed along our route. As we pass, each one of them does the same stupid clicky thing with the heels of their knee-high boots.

I'm sure it's supposed to intimidate us, but I can't help a laugh escaping my lips at about the hundredth heel click, and Klein's face turns red in anger, though he says nothing.

When we finally arrive after fifteen full minutes of walking, it's at a large hatch with two very serious Jutzen Marines flanking the door with wicked-looking assault rifles. To my relief, they don't point the guns at me or my men, but our escorts do make it extremely clear that I am to enter the room *alone*.

At first, Quinn looks very much like he's going to argue the point, but he and Paul aren't armed, and by the looks on the faces of the two Marines, they're probably looking for an excuse to take my guys out. So, I throw the big man a pleading look and I see the moment he relents. I try not to let my own relief show too plainly.

Leaving Quinn and Paul behind to stare daggers back at the two Jutzen Marines, I enter the hatch that Lieutenant Klein holds open and try not to wince when I hear it shut and lock behind me.

I find myself in a large room dominated by an expansive wood table. With space *and* mass at a premium on any warship, it's an extravagance I've never seen before in my own Navy and reminds me a little of the massive wood doors to my father's office on Skytran Orbital. Except that that was a space station, and this is a ship, so the impracticality and expense of this table dwarfs my father's doors.

At the far end of the table, a man stands from his seat as I enter. He's older, with graying hair and a lined face, and he's wearing a dress uniform festooned with ribbons and medals—kind of funny given that I know enough of the history of the Collective to know they haven't fought an actual battle with anyone in over a hundred years. Who would they fight? They're bordered on three sides by the might of the Leeward Republic and on the other by a smattering of independent systems, including Carter's World, with no navies to speak of. And not even most pirates are crazy enough to try and operate in Nazi space.

Regardless, I don't let my expression convey my disdain for the fruit salad on the guy's chest; instead, I nod respectfully. Etiquette probably requires that I salute, but I don't think I could bring myself to do so with *any* Jutzen officer. In fact, given that I'm Asian *and* a woman, I'm actually surprised the admiral is even willing to dine with me. I can't fathom how there are still fools in this galaxy that believe in some sort of master race and superior gender.

He doesn't take offense at my lack of decorum, at least not so I can see. He bows slightly and motions toward a seat on one side of the table, close to his own. "Welcome, Commander Lin," he says in a smooth voice with only a hint of the fake German accent I've heard that many Jutzen officers try to adopt. "Won't you please join me for dinner?"

"I would be honored," I say, though I feel anything but. Still, I don't want to show too much disrespect. The man may be part of what is essentially a cult of hate, but he *does* have a ship that could swat mine out of the sky without a thought.

He waits for me to be seated before he seats himself. "I am Vizeadmiral Otto Heinrich," he says as another hatch opens and two white-clad servants enter carrying trays of food. "It is my pleasure to welcome you to my flagship, *SMS Brandenburg*. I was extremely gratified to find your ship here on my routine patrol of this system. I have long wanted to meet you after the events of Gerson reached my ears. And may I say that I was extremely pleased to hear that rumors of your death in that battle were…exaggerated."

"Routine patrol?" I ask, ignoring his reference to Gerson. "I didn't think Capaldi was part of the Collective." The statement is a risky one, but if he thinks he can unbalance me with his false polite chit chat, I'm almost itching to show him that he can't.

Still, it's to my relief that he once again does not appear to take offense. "Of course, of course," he says with a smile and a dismissive wave of one hand. "Let us say that the citizens of Capaldi have yet to officially include themselves in the growing number of systems who bask in the light of the Fuhrer, but they do benefit from our unofficial protection, especially given the large community of Jutzen Collective emigrants who have chosen to settle in this beautiful system."

Whoa. That's news to me. And I wonder what my old King or even the Leeward Republic Congress must think of a Jutzen outpost—even an informal one—this close to their space, assuming they know. I want to press him for more details, but I'm interrupted by one of the servants placing a large plate before me full of steaming hot seafood.

Seafood? On a warship? Like the table, it's a gross extravagance, and from the smile on Heinrich's face, he knows what I'm thinking. But he says nothing, instead spearing a piece of lobster with his fork, dipping it in a cup of melted butter, and then bringing it to his lips.

Mentally shrugging, I do much the same, though I start with the shrimp—they've always been my favorite. And despite my surroundings, the first taste of the succulent food makes me realize how hungry I actually am right now. There hasn't been a ton of time to eat the last few weeks, and I've been largely avoiding food beyond simple rations, given how upset my stomach has generally been. But at the first taste of the richly-flavored shrimp, I am suddenly ravenous.

For several minutes, we eat, and the only talking is the occasional suggestion of things to try on my plate from Heinrich, which I politely nod along to. Finally, however, he pushes his plate away from him and settles back in his chair. I'm still hungry, but I sense that not following suit would likely take away the veneer of civility with which he is approaching this interaction. So I also, reluctantly, push my plate away and meet his steely gaze.

Have you ever heard that expression about someone's smile not reaching their eyes? It always used to annoy me when I read that in books because it just never made sense to me. How can someone smile or frown with just their eyes? Except now I get it. Because despite his seemingly warm smile, if I were to cover the bottom half of Heinrich's face, the top half would most certainly *not* convey anything in the realm of friendliness.

"Now, let us arrive at the reason I have invited you to visit my ship," he says frankly. I hold my tongue, not sure what good a response would do at this point. "I know you have come to Capaldi looking for Captain Brad Mendoza. It is my solemn and unfortunate duty to inform you that the captain is, in fact, dead."

He pauses, and if he's looking for a reaction from

me, he's not disappointed. I imagined a lot of different ways this conversation could go in my head, but none like this, and I know that my shock and sudden grief are clearly visible in the seconds it takes me to process his words and then school my emotions. He's a Nazi, I remind myself, and I can't trust him. He must be lying. I wish I could fully believe that.

"Three days ago," he says, "*Brandenburg* came across a small ship full of mercenaries in the outer system. They ignored our orders to submit to a routine safety inspection and fired on us without provocation. Needless to say, their ship was destroyed as a precautionary measure. When we examined the wreckage, we found the body of a man matching Captain Mendoza's description. I am sorry that you must find out this way about his untimely death, and I sincerely regret that we were unable to save him from his captors."

He pauses, obviously expecting a response or another reaction from me. But I feel suddenly cold inside…

"May I examine the body?" I ask in a robotic voice. "There are certain rites in the Promethean Navy for a dead officer. I would like to perform them and put him to rest."

The admiral takes on a pained look. "I regret that it is too late for that, Fraulein. You see, we already committed his remains, along with the other bodies found in the wreckage, to the depths of space, giving *him* full Jutzen military honors in the process, a courtesy we did not extend to the others, for obvious reasons, I think."

I consider this for a moment, my emotions warring

inside of me. "I see. Then I thank you, Vice Admiral, for your consideration toward my former captain. As you can imagine, I would like to return to my ship to grieve his loss." I look down at the table, not meeting his eyes.

"Of course, Korvettenkapitan," he responds. Then he surprises me by reaching out and using his fingers to lift my chin. I bite back an angry invective at the liberties he's taking, but only barely. He studies my face for a long moment.

"Such a pity," he says somberly, "for such a beautiful face to be ruined by such ugly scars. You must allow my ship's doctor to treat you while we are here. I guarantee he can do a better job than those near-savages on Carter's World."

I swallow the next angry response that comes to mind and instead lower my eyes. "I thank you again, Vice Admiral, for your kind offer. But I am afraid that I must decline. Now that our captain is dead, I must console my crew and return them to their planet. We will leave in a day after we are finished resupplying our ship."

He removes his hand from underneath my chin and nods. "I understand, Fraulein. *Brandenburg* stands ready to escort you from the system when you are prepared. Word of your engagement with pirates near the jump point reached us just hours ago, and I would never forgive myself if you ran afoul of them again on your way out of this system."

Two minutes later, a smug-looking Lieutenant Klein and his other unnamed officer friend escort Quinn, Paul, and me back to the shuttle. The return trip takes less than five minutes and appears to be on a much more direct route. We pass few crewmembers on our way this time.

Quinn looks at me the entire way with a questioning gaze. But I hold my tongue both during the walk back to our shuttle and during the short ride back to Capaldi Station. Only after we've safely reached *Persephone* do I allow myself to relax enough to speak.

"What happened in there, Commander?" he asks.

"The admiral told me that Captain Mendoza is dead."

The big man's face takes on a pained and sympathetic look, but I shake my head quickly. "And in doing so, he confirmed for me that Brad is alive."

Now Quinn looks confused, so I quickly explain.

"He said that his ship inadvertently killed the Captain when the small mercenary ship he was on fired on *Brandenburg* three days ago. But if Kayla and her crew were really dead, then why would Poulter try to stop us in the outer system? Because it was clear the guy wasn't just doing it for revenge. And when I told Poulter it was Kayla who killed his brother, his reaction wasn't about a woman who was already dead and gone.

"Not to mention, Heinrich knew I was treated for my burns on Carter's World. I'm sure he was trying to impress and intimidate me with his knowledge, but the only way he could know about that is if he spoke with someone who was *there* when I nearly died."

"Kayla," Quinn says, and I nod.

"We're being played, Quinn. Somehow, the Jutzens are in on this, and they just did their best to warn us off, which means the stakes just got much, much higher."

He thinks for a few seconds, digesting all that I just dumped on him. Then he meets my gaze steadily and nods once. "OK. What are we going to do about it?"

I give a tight-lipped smile in response. "Tell me, have you ever hijacked a space station?"

# TWENTY-THREE
## SPIN CYCLE

### *JESSICA LIN*

For two full years following my fall from grace at Hothan and Yolandra, I was assigned to desk duty on a station in the Lightman system. Even though I was a traitor, Promethean Naval Intelligence never allowed my case to make it to a court martial or even into the official record. Instead, they were convinced I would be more valuable to them if they used me to convey *false* information to my dear father and, by extension, to the Leeward Republic.

They turned out to be wrong. Jackson Hwong never reached out to me again, at least until two months ago when he had *Dauntless* board *Wanderer* in the Fiori system, and he never even responded to any of my half-hearted attempts to reestablish communication at the behest of my handlers over the years.

By the time Naval Intelligence figured out I was useless to them as an asset, enough time had passed that it would have been too embarrassing for them to suddenly put me on trial for the actions that led to the loss of the convoy at Yolandra. So, instead, as a punishment, they simply let me rot doing desk duty.

Naval administrative work on a space station is the most boring duty a combat officer can possibly pull. I worked nine-to-five most days, doing little more than processing the endless paperwork that, next to coffee, is the fuel of any Navy. Unfortunately, that left me with far too many hours free to reflect on what I'd done at Hothan and what had happened at Yolandra as a result, so I did my best to stay busy. For me, that meant going over every centimeter of the station I was assigned to and familiarizing myself with the way each and every one of its systems worked.

And luckily for me, space station design is a pretty standard thing. Sure, there are local variations, but once humanity finds something that works, we pretty much run with it and mass-produce it like crazy.

Capaldi Station is a lot like Lightman Station in both design and systems. So, by the next morning, when Uvalde and a very haggard-looking Illian finally return to *Persephone*, I'm ready to implement another truly foolish plan. But this time, even Quinn likes it.

"Paul," I say silently through my implant comm. "You ready?"

"Oorah, Commander," comes his reply. I've learned that the second largest member of Quinn's team used to be a Leeward Republic Marine, and he still talks and acts like one.

"Quinn, ready?" I ask on a different channel.

"When you are, Skipper," he says, calling me the honorific name usually reserved only for the most beloved captains. It's strangely moving to hear him say it, but I shove that to the back of my mind because timing on this is everything.

"Paul, go," I say back on the original channel. And suddenly, the space visible on the external camera feed on *Persephone's* main viewscreen starts to shift.

You see, most orbital stations can be controlled from one of two places. The first is the main command center, which is usually buried deep in the middle of the station where it's well-protected from the cold dark of space and any attacks, much like a warship's bridge. Storming and taking over a major station's command center is next to impossible unless you have a full division of Marines or even SEALs. It also takes a *lot* of time because there are about a hundred pressure bulkheads that can slam shut and bar your path on the way.

But the second place from which a station can be controlled is a much softer target. Every station has a traffic control center, usually called 'traffcon' for short, almost always placed at the very top of the station, with real transparent windows to help the controllers direct traffic even in the event of a sensor failure. And since most of a station's critical functions *can't* be controlled from traffcon, it tends to be far less secure than the main command center.

In fact, about the only thing you *can* do from traffcon, besides calling ships and assigning docking bays,

SKYLER RAMIREZ

is make moderate adjustments to the station's orientation using its thrusters. This redundant control resides in the traffic control center in case controllers need to shift a station slightly to enable docking with a damaged ship that can't make its own course or attitude adjustments.

Exactly five minutes ago, Paul and two of Quinn's other shooters practically waltzed into Capaldi Station's traffcon, quickly subdued and tied up the four civilian controllers in the room, and then preprogrammed a single position change into the station's thruster controller. Then, they waited for my signal.

Now, with my go-ahead, Paul triggers the preprogrammed command and he and his two shooters hoof it back as quickly as they can through the station to return to *Persephone's* docking gate. By the time station security figures out who triggered the command, they should be safely back on board.

There's a lot that can go wrong with our plan, but I breathe out in relief as the station starts rotating slowly. Ten minutes later, just as Paul and his team arrive back onboard, and just as the station rotates far enough that *Persephone* is no longer visible from Vice Admiral Heinrich's *Brandenburg*, Quinn throws a switch at the airlock and manually disengages our docking clamps. At the same time, Chief Jensen fires the thrusters—at twenty percent, *way* too much for an undocking procedure; Brad would be proud—and we barely wait until we're the proper distance away before he also kicks on the main drive.

The result is that *Persephone* is now burning at nearly full military power away from *Brandenburg*, but the mass of Capaldi Station is between us and the Jutzen battleship. With a little bit of luck, we manage to disappear over the planet's horizon before *Brandenburg* can emerge from behind the station and get a lock on our position.

## TWENTY-FOUR
# DIVE! DIVE! DIVE!

### *JESSICA LIN*

Of course, we're not out of the woods yet. A large battleship like *Brandenburg* has massive engines that mean its acceleration, while slower than that of a nimble corvette like *Persephone*, is still respectably high. So, our next move is key.

"Take us to the South Pole," I tell Jensen. It's a calculated risk. Capaldi Station orbits above the planet Christos at its equator. But Heinrich won't assume that we ran in that direction. He'll know that I will purposefully take a different course to try and throw him off, keeping the planet between me and him until I can get enough speed to slingshot away and hopefully put enough distance behind me that he won't be able to get a weapons lock.

He can prevent me from doing that even if he's only *close* to being on my tail when I try to escape orbit because a battleship has a *huge* weapons range. Of course, if he's in the wrong hemisphere when I leave orbit, then all bets are off for him because he'll still have the planet in his way.

So, he'll have to roll the dice and pick either the northern or the southern hemisphere to search first. And I'm willing to bet he picks the North for two reasons. First, even after millennia of living and working in space, humans still tend to think in terms of 'up' and 'down' versus a system plane, and we tend to go up far more than down to avoid trouble as if we're still instinctually flying aircraft in an atmosphere. And second, because I now know where Brad is being held, and I'm willing to bet so does Heinrich, and a departure from the planet's northern hemisphere would get me there a lot faster.

For both those reasons, I go south instead. And my gamble pays off. By the time Heinrich realizes his mistake and brings *Brandenburg* into the southern hemisphere, *Persephone* is well away and 'down' from the planet, just outside the larger ship's weapons range, where our superior acceleration can *keep* us outside that range until we run out of fuel, and we topped ourselves off at the station using most of my remaining credits.

We allow ourselves a little celebration, but it's tempered by the simple fact that we are now moving almost directly *away* from the coordinates Uvalde was able to get us. We're running away from where Brad is.

## TWENTY-FIVE
# DID I MENTION I HATE NAZIS?

### *BRAD MENDOZA*

So, I guess this *entire* time, Heather Kilgore could have gotten free from her bindings whenever she wanted. She just didn't want to until now.

How rude.

The shouts outside our room died down after only a few hours, but Kayla and her evil minions are obviously still worked up enough that they've left us alone for what feels like about half a day. We've spent most of that time actually free of our bonds and crouching by the hatch, waiting to get the drop on the next person to check on us. It's been a horribly boring, if welcome, respite. But it startles us both awake when we finally do hear the hatch unlock from the outside. Our plan is elegant in its simplicity *and* its suicidal bravery. When the door opens, we're going to attack whoever opens it and then go for freedom.

See, suicidal. But it's better than nothing.

The hatch finally opens, and a big mercenary enters. He barely has time to show surprise that Kilgore and I aren't tied up on the floor across the room before I grab his ankles, and she jumps on his back and locks his arms to his sides.

He falls forward like a domino and, without his arms to break his fall, smashes his face right into the hard metal deck with a cry of pain. Kilgore leaps off of him and whirls to face the open door, with me following suit, albeit much more slowly.

Then she falls back with a cry as what I *hope* is a stun round slams into her chest from the pistol Kayla is holding. I try and leap toward my abuser, but she's much faster than me, and the last thing I feel before everything goes dark is my bladder releasing as thousands of volts of electricity course through me.

Fun.

When I wake up, I have a massive headache. I mean, I've had a headache pretty constantly since first waking up in this little cell, but this is *so* much worse.

Unfortunately, I can't do anything about it because I'm tied up again, though at least not on the floor. Instead, I'm on what I feels like a hard metal gurney. And I can turn my head just enough to see that Kilgore, also awake, is on a similar gurney next to me. Both of us have all sorts of fun little wires and tubes hooked up to our arms.

Apparently, it's time to use the Nazis' truth serum.

Kayla stands over me, smiling. "Brad, you're finally awake. Now, let's talk about those coordinates you owe me." And she pushes in a plunger on one of the IV tubes.

## TWENTY-SIX
# BALLISTIC

### *JESSICA LIN*

R emember how I talked about just how huge space is, even within a single star system? Well, the same principle that made it so unlikely we would ever find Brad in the expanse of the Capaldi system is now also the principle that will make it nearly impossible for *Brandenburg* to find us.

I hope.

In a perfect world, I would take my little ship halfway around the system and then approach Kayla's and Brad's location from the opposite direction that she and the *Brandenburg* will be expecting based on my vector away from Capaldi Station. But that would take the better part of a week, even at full burn, and Brad probably doesn't have that kind of time. The presence

SKYLER RAMIREZ

of a Jutzen battleship in the system is a pretty good
indication that things are quickly coming to a head.

So, once we're safely out of sensor range of *Brandenburg* and even the Christos planetary sensor network—
it pays to play it safe in some regards—we change
vector and burn for another six hours, this time straight
'up' in relation to the system plane. Then we shift
course again.

Now, we're on a ballistic course right toward the
coordinates Uvalde found for Brad's location at only a
slightly different angle from the one we would be on if
we'd just turned around straight and burned toward it.

Because even a warship's sensors are in large part
based on thermal signatures and EM radiation, I order
our main drive off, our reactor to minimum, and all
systems to standby except life support and passive
sensors. I effectively turn *Persephone* into little more
than a tiny, floating hunk of metal hurtling through the
vastness of a planetary system.

So, we wait. And that's the worst part because every
centimeter of me is itching to find and rescue my
captain, but there's absolutely nothing I can do to make
this go any faster.

"How sure are you of these coordinates?" I ask
Uvalde for probably the seventh time. It's a terrible
command move for me to keep asking her—it conveys
a lack of trust in my people. But I can't help it right
now. And thankfully, she doesn't seem to take offense.

"As sure as I can be, boss," she says with a not-very-
confidence-inspiring shrug. "I figured they'd need
supplies, so I looked for ships coming in and leaving
the station multiple times over the last several weeks

from vectors not directly related to a jump point. I only found one that fit the bill, and it always headed back in the same direction. The rest I just figured out by standard flight times."

I nod again because she's told me all of this several times now. And as much as I wish we had more to go on, I have to admit that it's the most solid intel we've had on Brad's location since we started looking. And it's not like it's just some random point in space, either. It's relatively close to a very small planet, though not an inhabited one, and *Persephone's* computer says there *used* to be an orbital platform there from the days when someone thought Capaldi would be a hub of trade between the Prometheans and the Republic.

Maybe the records are wrong, and that station is still there.

Finally, Robinson makes a high-pitched cry of triumph from the sensor station. "Commander! I think we found it!"

I allow myself a smile. I'm coming, Brad.

## TWENTY-SEVEN
# THE DUMBEST PLAN OF THEM ALL

*JESSICA LIN*

"We can't dock with the station. Even if they're running a skeleton crew, they'll have an alert setup if any of the airlocks trigger, though maybe they missed doing so for the emergency hatches. But either way, they'll see us if we get that close."

Illian's assessment is delivered in the same professional tone in which he delivers *everything*, but even he sounds at least a little exasperated beneath the surface. Because we are *so close* to our target right now, but Brad might as well be three systems away for all the good it does us.

"This only works if we can board them," I remind everyone, stating the obvious. The good news, if there is any, is that, as far as our passive sensors can determine, the station doesn't appear to have any weapons. And whatever supply ship they're using isn't visible either, at least on the side facing us.

However, we have two problems. The first is that our ballistic course won't take us close enough to the station to dock with it unless we fire off our main drive to adjust our vector. And they'll see us the second we do, even if they're not really paying attention. Second, Illian is right: there's *no* way Kayla and her mercenaries don't notice a ship docking with their station.

Either means that she'll have plenty of notice that we're there, both to defend against us *and* to likely kill Brad just out of spite before we can rescue him.

"Tell me again why a scrambler won't work?" Lieutenant Jericho asks. It's the first time he's ventured out of engineering long enough to join one of our little strategy sessions, and he looks uncomfortable being away from his engines for this long.

I open my mouth to answer, but Perry beats me to it. "Come on Lieutenant," she says in the tone of a grandmother lecturing a slow child, "disabling the station is as good as announcing we're here. And what do you think happens then? Either they kill Captain Mendoza outright, or we have ourselves a hostage situation. It's the same exact problem we'd have if we lit off the main drive right now and broadcast that we're coming."

"She's right," Quinn rumbles from his customary standing position by *Persephone's* wardroom door. "We have to do this fast and clean before they can react, or there's no way we get Captain Mendoza out of this alive."

I slam my open palm down on the table, causing

everyone in the room except Quinn to jump. "Chitoran Slide!" I cry out. They all look at me like I'm speaking another language.

I explain. "*Persephone*, unlike its namesake, has cold-reaction thrusters." Illian's eyes light up, but Quinn still looks confused, so I elaborate. "It means we can fire our thrusters to make course adjustments without creating a heat bloom. If we're lucky, they won't see us."

"You're right," Illian says, but then the excitement fades from his eyes, "so long as they only use passive sensors. But cold thrusters have their limits, and they won't get us all the way there. We'd still have to light off the main drive to close the gap, and I'm afraid they'd still have plenty of time to see us coming."

He's right, curse him, and my mind races for a reason to argue with him, but I find none.

But Quinn does. "How close could those thrusters get us before they're likely to notice us?"

Illian checks his implant, his eyes going out of focus for a moment. "Cold-reaction thrusters are low power," Illian says. "They'll move us, but only slowly. But the real danger is them seeing us once we get too close. Figure…"

He throws a number up onto his implant in share mode so we can all see it. My heart sinks. It's close, but not close enough to give us the element of surprise when we finally make a go at them.

"No way," Perry says what we're all thinking. "They'd have way too much time to react to our presence. Captain Mendoza would be dead before we finished docking."

It kills me how often we're talking about Brad's

impending death right now, but it's also oddly comforting because *all* of us are at least thinking in terms that he is still alive *now*. I won't even let myself consider the alternative.

"We do a SOSO jump," Quinn says, and we all turn to look at him.

"A what?" Illian asks. I just shake my head. I know exactly what Quinn is suggesting, and compared even to my idiotic move with the *Hawkwing*, it's absolutely *insane*.

"A SOSO jump," he explains, clearly getting excited. "Stands for Space Origin, Space Objective. SEALS do them in these types of situations."

"Are you seriously saying…" Illian trails off, apparently so incredulous he can't even finish his question.

"Yes," I say dryly, "Mr. Quinn wants to go outside on *Persephone's* hull in a vacsuit and *jump* from our ship onto the station."

Quinn just shrugs. "Piece of cake. That station's in a fixed orbit, and we're ballistic. If you can use the cold reaction thrusters to slow us down just a little while you also move us closer, the math says we'll be close enough to a zero-relative velocity intercept that our suit thruster packs can handle the rest. And those are small enough that they're unlikely to trigger the station's sensors."

We all look at him incredulously.

"What?" he says, looking hurt. "Just because I'm a shooter and I like to blow things up, I can't solve advanced mathematical equations? You do all know that building bombs requires a lot of precise calculations, right?"

I shrug. *I* was actually glaring at him because I still

think his plan is terrible. His math actually impresses me, especially when my own implant-assisted check shows he's right.

"I hate to say this, but it might just work, and it also might be our *only* option," Illian admits, giving the big man an appreciative nod and saying just about the *last* thing I would expect to hear from the normally cautious and by-the-book commander.

"We can't negotiate with them?" Harris suggests timidly from the other end of the table. I think most of us forgot he was even in the room.

I smile at him but shake my head. "No. We're pretty sure the Jutzens are working with Kayla if my lovely dinner with Heinrich is any indication. And *Brandenburg* can be here in just four hours at full burn, assuming she's not already en route. If she arrives before we get away, we're done. We can't fight a battleship. All Kayla needs to do is just hold out that long, and she'll know we won't fire at the station and risk Brad's life, so we really have nothing to threaten her with."

"So, no other options?" Quinn asks, and now he looks almost as giddy as a kid on Christmas day. That's...concerning.

But I heave a sigh of frustration and shake my head. "I can't think of any. Commander Illian, work with Chief Jensen to lay in a course and start firing the cold reaction thrusters. Let's close every meter of distance and shed every bit of velocity we think we can get away with. And Major Boyd," I turn to the big man, "you have exactly as much time as Commander Illian says that will take, to convince me beyond a shadow of a doubt that you *can* pull this off."

He smiles, but my next words make that turn into a deep frown.

"Because, Major, if you're doing this, then *I'm* going with you."

## TWENTY-EIGHT
# TRUTH SERUM

### *BRAD MENDOZA*

"And when I was five, I tried to tie the tails of two cats together and see what happened. Grandma spanked me so hard I cried for an hour."

I vaguely remember, as part of my SERE training, what they taught us about resisting chemically-enhanced interrogation. It was taught almost as an afterthought, as our implants are already programmed to counteract the effects of all known agents. But not this one. So, I'm doing what that training told me.

I'm telling the truth...in minute detail, starting from my earliest memories, talking nonstop over Kayla's attempts to ask me the question she's waited all this time to get an honest answer to.

Nevertheless, I can feel my control slipping, and it's

only a matter of time before she—and the Nazis—get their coordinates.

Because Heather Kilgore isn't doing much better, and I just had to listen to a really embarrassing story about her first kiss in junior high. I can tell she's slipping as much as I am by the way she keeps throwing desperate glances my way, probably now wishing she'd killed me when she had the chance.

We have hours at best before one or both of us crack.

# TWENTY-NINE
# THE STARS

### *JESSICA LIN*

"You've done this before, right?" I ask Quinn at the worst possible time. Not only have I already agreed to let him do the SOSO jump, but I'm literally strapped to the front of his vacsuit like a baby in a carrier because I *insisted* on going with him, and he just as emphatically refused to let me go any other way.

"Uh, once, on a training jump in the Republic Marines," he says sheepishly.

"How far?" I ask, dreading the answer.

"About five hundred meters."

Great, because we are *a lot* further than five hundred meters away.

I consider calling the whole thing off, but then I think of Brad, and I steel my nerves.

"Commander," Illian's voice breaks into our helmet comms. "We've reached closest approach. As soon as you give the all-clear, we'll hit full burn and meet you back here. Happy hunting."

The traditional naval send-off sends a surge of emotion through me, mostly good, but also terrifying... truly terrifying.

"All right," I manage to say anyway. "Major Boyd, we are a go."

"Roger," he replies. "Hit it!"

The outer airlock door blows open, and the over-pressured air we've pumped into it explodes out into space, propelling with it Quinn Boyd, Paul Hartman, Heddy Rodriguez...and me. The undamaged port airlock can only hold that many people, and Quinn's other three operators will need to wait for the air pumps to fill it again before they can follow us.

None of that really matters to me now because I'm about as frightened as I ever have been. Here I am, strapped to a guy who has only done this *once,* hurtling across the vastness of space with nothing but a thin helmet, a thinner suit, and Quinn's small thruster pack that's only meant for making small adjustments at low speeds. Not to mention that if we happen to *miss* the station, the gravity of the little planet it's orbiting will suck us down well before *Persephone* could ever hope to recover us.

I'm going to die, and the worst part is I won't even know I'm dead for several more hours because that's how long it will take for us to reach—or more likely, sail right by—Kayla's station. Assuming it even *is* Kayla's station because we still have no real verification of that.

And even if we do reach it, Brad is probably already dead. And even if he isn't…

I take a deep breath. I'm spiraling, and I know it, but knowing it and pulling myself out of it are two very different things. And not even Harris is here to talk me down, nor can I even communicate with Quinn while we're in strict comm blackout. But then I look, and I mean *really* look out the front of my helmet.

The stars are incredible. You would think that having spent my entire adult life in space, a starscape like this one would be commonplace to me. But warships don't have many windows, and even on civilian ships that do, like *Wanderer*, you spend most of your time looking at your instruments, not the stars outside.

Now, for perhaps the first time in my life, all I *can* do is look. And they are spectacular. Despite myself, I feel my breathing slow, and my heart rate settles down as I marvel at the expanse around us. I've never seen anything more beautiful in my life, and I'm suddenly overcome with a different emotion than fear, one that makes me choke up a little.

If I die, I would not be disappointed if this is the last sight I see.

## THIRTY
# GIVING UP AND GIVING IN

### BRAD MENDOZA

"Eight five seven three point two by six one eight…"

My heart sinks as Kayla finally gets the coordinates she's been looking for all this time. And that means the Nazis will get the stellarium.

Heather Kilgore finishes reciting the numbers. It's surprising, I suppose, that she broke first. But maybe not so much. When you're a high and mighty Agent of the King's Cross, you probably spend your entire life feeling pretty invincible. Being captured like this and tortured and then hopped up on truth serum is undoubtedly a very rude awakening for Kilgore. For me, I had far less distance to fall—softer landing. And I had a lot more in the way of personal reasons to not give my captors anything.

"About time," hisses Kayla with a predatory grin. "Jerod, transmit these to *Brandenburg* immediately and tell them we're ready for them to come and pick us up."

She turns and exits the room along with Jerod—Norm—and leaves Kilgore and me alone in our cell, still strapped to our hard metal gurneys.

"Wow, you folded quicker than I thought," I say, knowing as I do so that it's an extremely insensitive thing to say, but literally being unable to stop myself because it is, after all, the truth. And I am, after all, full of truth serum.

"And you held out far longer than I thought," she says back morosely. "How did *you* hold out longer than me?"

I ignore the implied insult and instead try to shrug, but I'm tied too tightly to the gurney, so I cock my head to hopefully convey the same general emotion. "Easy," I say, "I never knew the coordinates."

I'm looking over at her, and now she turns her head to stare at me, mouth agape.

"But...at Fiori, I thought..."

I try and shrug again. It doesn't work...again. "Yeah, you and everyone else. I keep telling people I can't do math in my head anymore; why would any of you think I can remember a bunch of random numbers just because I saw them *once*?"

"So, all this time, you were bluffing?" She asks it with such incredulity that I can't help but laugh...or maybe that's because I'm high as a kite.

"Yeah," I say between snickers. "I only ever knew the fake coordinates you gave me, and those only because I saved them on my implant. I would have totally forgotten them otherwise."

Heather Kilgore stares at me for another moment while I start laughing again. Then she starts laughing, too. It feels kind of good, you know, if we can forget for a moment that we just doomed the entire Fringe to subjugation by war-happy Nazis.

"Captain Mendoza," she gasps between laughs, "you are the biggest idiot I've ever met. But maybe the gutsiest man as well."

I'm equally offended and pleased by her statement because it has to be the truth.

# THIRTY-ONE
# A HAPPY LANDING...
# HOPEFULLY

### *JESSICA LIN*

I see a gloved hand hold up a single finger in front of my helmet. It's Quinn telling me we're about one hour out from—hopefully—landing on the target station. I really want to ask him if we're on course, but I can't, so I settle back sullenly and try to scan the space in front of me for any sight of the station itself against the backdrop of its small host planet.

I see nothing. It's not encouraging.

Still, there's nothing to do but wait, and I'm close enough now to the execution of the next phase of the plan that I keep my mind focused on that and stave off the spiraling emotions that otherwise threaten to drag me down.

Just another hour, Brad. I'm coming.

# THIRTY-TWO
# BONDING

### *BRAD MENDOZA*

"He really likes cornflakes."

"Really?" I ask Kilgore. "But they're so bland. I would think he could eat anything he wants. Why cornflakes?"

"I don't know," she says, giggling. "But King Charles makes sure that the palace is always stocked with boxes and boxes of cornflakes. I heard they ran out once, and he almost fired half the kitchen staff."

I can't help but picture in my head a red-faced King Charles the Eighth of the Royal House of Worthington, Defender of the Realm, and Lord of the Federated Systems of Prometheus...throwing a spoon at some servants because they ran out of his favorite breakfast cereal. Now I'm giggling hysterically along with Kilgore.

"And what about the Queen?" I ask when we both finally come up for air. We've been in this room for several hours since Kayla took the coordinates and left, and the effects of the truth serum, if anything, have only gotten more powerful. I think she forgot to turn off the flow when she bounced off to tell the Nazis the good news about their plans for galactic conquest.

"The Queen hates cornflakes," Kilgore says. Then she lowers her voice conspiratorially, "But she *loves* the palace gardener, sometimes as often as four times a week!"

This causes us both to devolve into another bout of laughter.

"And what about you? Any juicy secrets to share?" Kilgore asks me when she can once again speak.

"Well, did you ever hear about the time Vice Admiral Nelson's prize beagle got launched in an escape pod down to the surface of Kipling IV?"

Her eyes widen. "Yes! That was *you*?"

I nod, though I'm mildly insulted she would simply assume that. "It wasn't my fault, really. I was on my snotty cruise, and I had orders to do a test launch of an escape pod as part of the carrier's annual safety certification. How was I supposed to know that I was choosing the pod that the little dog liked to sleep in?"

She laughs hysterically, and I join in. Then she stops and eyes me again. "Wait, how did you *not* get sent to Gerson back then for that little stunt?"

"Let's just say that my commanding officer was extremely worried that the admiral would punish him along with me, so he noted the launch as a malfunction in the log. Nelson was pissed, but he didn't have anyone to blame except himself for letting that dog roam the ship unsupervised."

"Captain Mendoza," Kilgore says with a wide grin, "if you have more stories like that, then we might just have some fun before they kill us."

I laugh, and she laughs. For some reason, *everything* is hilarious to us right now, even our impending deaths.

## THIRTY-THREE
# LIKE A LEAF

*JESSICA LIN*

A SOSO jump is the equivalent of shooting a bullet at another bullet and hoping you hit it softly enough to not go splat. Luckily, despite his lack of actual experience and practice, Quinn turns out to be pretty good at this, and by the time we reach Kayla's station, we're moving so slowly that we land like a leaf on the wind. The same goes for the other two shooters, Paul and Heddy, who are, after all, tethered to Quinn.

Now we just have to wait for the second half of our boarding party. By Quinn's calculations, they should be about ten minutes behind us, assuming they didn't get off course. We won't know, unfortunately, until we see them…or we don't.

Somehow, these ten minutes feel longer than the seven hours in transit. Because Brad is just on the other side of this hull, I know it! And every second we wait is a second I'm convinced is his last if we don't hurry!

190

## THIRTY-FOUR
# MISSING QUITE A PARTY

### *BRAD MENDOZA*

I'm laughing at another story about the King from Heather Kilgore when I hear a really funny sound. It's like a pop. And then someone screams like they just got thrown a surprise party.

Then I hear more pops, so I'm pretty sure someone is lighting off fireworks. I wish they'd let us come out of our cell and see the show. It sounds really fun.

"Hey, guess what!" I call over to Kilgore. "I peed myself when they shot me with that stun round."

"No way!" she calls back. "So did I."

We start laughing again, doing our best to not be sad about not getting invited to what sounds like a really great party going on out in the corridor.

## THIRTY-FIVE
# BATTLE ROYALE

### JESSICA LIN

I hired Quinn Boyd and his team as shooters over a week ago, but I've never actually seen them shoot anything up until this moment.

I can see now that they are worth every penny I spent and promised them and more, because they are incredible. Kayla's crew may be made up of mercenaries and may outnumber us four-to-one, but they don't stand a chance against Quinn and his other five shooters. I'm just trying to stay out of their way at this point. We must have killed half of Kayla's mercenaries before they even knew we were here, using the silenced weapons Quinn's team brought. Only now is the enemy starting to actually shoot back.

I'm moving in a crouch behind Heddy, who is in the middle of our four-man formation with Quinn out in front and Paul walking backward to cover our rear. A mercenary leans around the corner of an intersection in the corridor ahead of us and squeezes off a shot that goes wide. Quinn's doesn't, and the man doesn't fire again as Quinn's bullet takes him in the forehead and sends him falling backward and down into the corridor.

Behind me, I hear Paul's gun spit twice in such rapid succession that it sounds like only one shot. I look back to see another mercenary, this one a woman I actually recognize as one of the fake militia members from our assault on the pirates in Carter's System, slump to the deck, dead. That's OK; I didn't like her much back then, either.

We reach the intersection, and there's a click on our helmet comms as two of Quinn's other three shooters approach the same intersection from a perpendicular corridor.

"Clear," calls out Forbes, a small, wiry man with a buzz cut who speaks even more rarely than Heddy.

"Clear," responds Quinn. "Adams?"

Forbes just shakes his head, and I feel like someone punched me in the stomach. I knew there was a pretty good chance not all of us would survive, but the first death of a member of our crew hits me hard.

The six of us who remain—five shooters and one ex-Navy commander who has no business being here—briefly stop in the intersection, Quinn's people taking position covering us down each corridor, even the two already declared clear, just in case.

"That way leads back to the docking airlocks," Paul says in the comm. We haven't taken our helmets off, just in case Kayla's people decide to evacuate the air in our part of the station. "If there's a prisoner, probably more likely they're that way, toward central control," he continues, pointing down the other corridor. I try to ignore the fact that he just said 'if'.

"Oorah," Quinn says to confirm, and off we go, now with two shooters out in front and two in the rear, with me still sandwiched in the middle with Heddy.

We round a bend in the corridor to find a closed hatch with two guards standing nervously outside. They don't even have time to react before Quinn and Paul put them down. Then, the two shooters each take up position on either side of the hatchway while Heddy opens the latch and pushes on the hatch. Quinn and Paul dart through the opening in quick sequence with Heddy fast on their heels, and I hear several pops from inside.

"Commander," Heddy's voice calls over the comm. "Target secured."

My heart leaps in my chest because those words can only mean one thing! Without waiting for Quinn's OK, I bolt through the hatchway and stop short inside as I take it all in.

Blood splatters the bulkheads and deck everywhere, though it seems to be a mixture of both fresh and dried crimson. Two fresh bodies are near the door, and I recognize both of them. One was the man I knew as Norman Smith, the fake militia leader on Carter's World. The other is the fake President Carter. In the center of the room, I see Kayla standing with her hands up and a scowl on her face, but I ignore her. To either side of her are metal gurneys. On one is a woman I recognize, though I can't immediately place her. And on the other is what looks like a skeleton with loose skin and a long, scraggly beard...

I rush to Brad's side, simultaneously relieved beyond measure and horrified as I reach him. He looks almost nothing like the man I last saw in Carter's System five weeks ago. Not only does he appear horribly malnourished, but his sagging skin is covered in welts, cuts, and bruises. He's even missing a finger, only a dirty bandage tied where it once was. As I look down at him, he stares back at me with unfocused, sunken eyes.

Realizing he probably can't see me well through the glare of my vacsuit helmet, I reach up and undo the clasp and then whip it off, and my nose is assaulted by the mixed sour smell of urine and the metallic aroma of blood. But I don't care, and I reach down and lay my hand on his cheek.

"Jess?" he asks, his voice scratchy but still the voice I remember, and I'm filled with indescribable joy at hearing my name on his lips. "You're alive!" he says with the excitement of a little boy. "What happened to your face?"

My joy sinks. I almost allowed myself to forget about my disfigurement, and I'm suddenly irrationally self-conscious about the way I must look to him. When we last met, he couldn't take his eyes off of me—though he probably thought I didn't notice—and now...

"You're the most beautiful thing I've ever seen," he says, his voice full of wonder, and the joy surges back. "And the scars look *so* cool."

"Well, *I* think you look terrible," another voice

intrudes, and I look over at the woman tied to the other gurney. That red hair…

"Agent Kilgore?" I ask in surprise. "What are you doing here?"

"I," she says, sounding almost drunk, "came here to kill Brad so he couldn't tell anyone the coordinates of the stellarium deposit in the Gerson system. But Brad's an idiot and didn't even know the coordinates. I did. And *I* told them, so mission failed. And now Brad and I are full of truth serum, and I'm pretty sure we're best friends now."

I shake my head to clear it because I'm certain I didn't hear her right. Brad didn't know the coordinates this entire time? And truth serum? I thought that was just a myth.

"Yeah, no," Brad says, giggling. "I may be *your* best friend, but you're not *mine*. Jessica is my best friend. I love her *so* much."

OK, now this is getting extremely weird, but I'm so happy to find Brad alive that I decide to ignore it and just let myself be equal parts overjoyed and relieved.

"You're too late," a scornful voice breaks into my celebratory thoughts, and I look up to see Kayla, now against one wall where Heddy is searching her for weapons, and Paul is pointing his assault rifle right at her head. "We already sent the coordinates, and the *Brandenburg* is on its way here now."

I sigh. That's bad news all around.

"Hey, Jess. Kayla really sucks. Did I mention I love you?" Brad chimes in, sounding like a first-grader who ate a little too much glue.

I shrug. "You know, Brad, you're right. Kayla does

suck." I smile down at him, and then I squeeze his hand and walk over to where Heddy has Kayla up against the wall, and she's now cuffed her hands behind her."

"Come to shoot me, you little trollop?" she sneers. "Or should I call you something different now, you deformed, two-faced little—"

Kayla doesn't get to finish whatever insult she was going to throw my way. My fist connecting solidly with her jaw cuts her off, and my knee to her stomach prevents her from saying anything else. She slumps to the deck, and Heddy grins at me.

"Told you she's a ninja!" Brad says triumphantly to Kilgore behind me.

## THIRTY-SIX
# THE NAZIS ARE COMING!

*JESSICA LIN*

"Commander, we'll be alongside in ten minutes," Illian's voice says in my helmet comm. At this point, we're in full control of the station, but we're all together with our few prisoners near the airlock just in case we missed someone. On the sensor feed relayed from *Persephone*, I can see our ship doing her deceleration burn after her sprint toward us.

Unfortunately, I can also see another ship on the feed: *Brandenburg*. The Nazis will be in weapons range in less than thirty minutes.

"Hurry, Francis," I tell Illian. "We don't have much time."

"We'll make it," Brad assures me. He's sitting on a chair someone found for the purpose, a blanket around his shoulders and a cup of coffee held gingerly in his hands. His mind has largely cleared; once we got them disconnected from the IVs, both he and Kilgore quickly sobered up. She's in a similar chair a few meters down the corridor where she won't get in the way, but I insisted that Brad be right next to me; I'm not planning on letting him out of my sight for...well, maybe forever.

I look down at him now, and he blushes. "Listen, Jessica, about what I said in there..."

"Brad, shut up," I say, grinning at him so there's no sting in my words. "How about we talk about your profession of undying love *after* we escape from the Nazis?"

He blushes even deeper red now, and I have to try hard to suppress a giggle. We're not out of the woods yet, but just having him here with me makes everything seem possible, including making a clean getaway.

"So," I say, changing the subject, "you're sure the Jutzens already have the coordinates?"

He nods. "Positive. I heard Kayla ordering her men to comm them the instant Kilgore gave them up."

I still can't believe it was Kilgore, the invincible Agent of the King's Cross, who spilled the exact location of the stellarium deposit in Gerson, but I guess that truth serum must be serious stuff.

"But they're still burning toward us," I say soberly.

Brad frowns. "I imagine they don't want to leave any witnesses to warn Prometheus they're coming."

"*MV Persephone*, this is *SMS Brandenburg*," a new voice, brimming over with arrogance, comes through my helmet comm, relayed by Illian from our ship. "Do not attempt to dock with the station, or we will destroy you *and* the station."

I look at Brad and raise my eyebrows. He grins back at me. "Any stupid plans come to mind?" I ask.

He laughs, and it's the most wonderful sound in the world to me despite our situation. "That's your department, Jess. I'm all out of stupid."

## THIRTY-SEVEN
# GETTING OUT OF DODGE

*JESSICA LIN*

I llian executes what might be the most perfect and certainly the fastest docking maneuver I've ever seen. The ten minutes he promised turn to eight, and within fifteen, we've completely transferred over to *Persephone* and we cast off the docking clamps.

Before I even make it to the bridge, Illian has already lit off the main drive and started the ship running directly away from the oncoming *Brandenburg*, keeping the station between us and them just as we did back at Christos. My opinion of the wiry commander from Carter's World continues to rise daily, and I feel a pang of odd regret that the mission that brought us together is now all but over. I'm sure that he and the others will be returning to their home planet, and it won't feel the same on *Persephone's* bridge without them.

"Commander!" Illian cries as I enter the bridge with Brad right behind me, the latter supported between Quinn and Heddy. "We have a problem."

I focus on him. Of course, something would have to go wrong!

"There's a sputter in the main drive," he explains. "We must have taken more damage than we thought in the battle with *Hawkwing*. We've got Jericho and his engineers working on it, but he says anything above seventy percent thrust, and we're likely to lose the drive altogether."

Uh oh. That's not good.

"What does that do to our escape from *Branden-burg*?" I ask him, though I think I already know the answer.

Illian frowns. "They only have a twelve percent edge in acceleration on us now, but they're carrying a lot of speed already, and the station's orbit had us moving *toward* them, so we're overcoming a negative relative velocity. Bottom line, they'll be in weapons range in fifteen minutes and at their angle of approach, we won't get around the planet's horizon before then."

It's *a lot* worse than I thought, and I feel a sudden anger rise in me. I have *not* come this far to lose now! Then I look over at Brad and feel a surge of hope. "What do you think, Captain?" I ask him, motioning for Quinn and Heddy to deposit him in the command chair in the center of the bridge.

Brad looks at me from his sunken eyes and slowly shakes his head, digging his heels into the deck before the two shooters can move him any further. I knit my eyebrows in confusion, not understanding, and then I realize that the entire bridge has gone dead quiet. Looking around, I see every one of the officers and crew looking between Brad and me in a strange, breathless anticipation.

"Sorry, Jess," Brad says, the exhaustion of the last five weeks heavy in his voice, but his tone is as firm and unyielding as I've ever heard it. "I'm not the captain."

I cock my head to one side. "What are you talking about? Of course, you're the captain."

He shakes his head and smiles at me, and I see a glimmer of the old Brad through the scraggly over-grown beard and the gaunt face. He can barely stand, even supported between the two shooters, but he shakes them off anyway and balances precariously on one foot, favoring the other one.

"Look at all this, Jess," he says, wonder in his voice. "A warship with a crew as good as any I've ever seen, venturing into enemy territory and executing the most daring rescue I've ever heard of. That was *you*, Jess. *You.* Not me. I'm not the smartest guy alive, or even in this room, but even I can see that there's only one captain for the new *Persephone*."

He draws himself up as far as he can on one leg, straightening his back and raising his right arm in a sharp salute. "Orders, Captain Lin?"

I stand there, stunned, not knowing whether to scream at him to stop being an idiot or marvel at what he just said. Then I look around at the bridge crew again. One by one, starting with Illian, they get up from their seats and stand at perfect attention, giving me salutes equal to the one Brad just gave me. Even Uvalde stands up from her customary place on the deck and throws me a sloppy two-fingered salute while Quinn and Heddy grin and put their right fists over their hearts in the traditional Leeward Republic Marine salute.

Unbidden, tears spring to my eyes, and a sense of gratitude for this crew and these men and women rises up inside of me, unequaled by any I've felt since I ruined my life on *Ordney*. And suddenly, I feel an overwhelming sense of...home.

"Orders, Captain Lin?" Illian asks, repeating Brad's question.

I shake myself and focus on him, meeting his gaze, and find in it a steadiness that I need right now. "Commander," I say to him. "Let's get that planet between us and *Brandenburg* as quickly as we can and target a barrage of ship-to-ship missiles on that station. I want to start a fire."

## THIRTY-EIGHT
# THE MOST BEAUTIFUL WOMAN IN THE GALAXY

### *BRAD MENDOZA*

Once, back on the original *Persephone*, when I first saw Jessica take charge and come up with the daring plan to take out that Koratan destroyer, I remember thinking that she was the most beautiful woman I'd ever seen, especially when she was confident and happy.

Now…she's positively radiant, and I'm riveted watching her interact with the crew—*her* crew. Gone entirely is the timid woman I met in the Gerson system. Gone is the uncertainty she's carried in herself since her mistake in the Hothan system. Gone is the old Jessica Lin that I fell in love with. What I'm seeing now is an entirely new person, and I didn't think it was even possible to love someone more than I already did her, but I find myself entranced and captivated by her now in ways that I wouldn't have believed could exist a few days ago.

"Cheng," she barks confidently on the intercom down to engineering. "Jericho, how long could we go full burn before that stutter becomes a real problem?"

"Uncertain," comes the harried response. "The drive could blow the second we ramp it up, or it could give us an hour or two before it blows. But it *will* blow if we leave it on full military power."

"Cheng, you're going to find a way to give me thirty minutes when I say so. Because if you don't, we're dead anyway. Understood?" The way she says it brooks no argument, and the man instantly acknowledges her order and signs off to go and work with his small engineering crew.

"Commander, we ready on that missile spread?" she barks at the guy named Illian.

"Yes, Captain. On your command," he replies crisply.

"OK, people," she says, "here's what we're going to do."

As she explains the plan, I see eyebrows raise across the bridge, first in disbelief, then in understanding, then in excitement. Because it's quite possibly the craziest plan any of us have ever heard, and that's saying something! But it also just might be the *only* plan that can work, assuming we get a little bit of dumb luck to go with it.

I'm watching the interplay, still captivated by my

XO…no, my *captain*, when the short green-haired Latina woman I saw when I first entered the bridge comes over and plops down on the deck next to the empty bridge engineering station I'm sitting at.

"Hola, chico," she says with a sly grin. "So, you're the hombre that all this fuss is about?"

I nod, not really sure how to read the woman.

She looks me up and down and then shrugs. "You don't look like much, chico. Not sure what the Captain was all worked up about. Way she was looking for you, I figured you must be the most guapo hombre in the galaxy." She wrinkles up her nose in disgust. "Or at least a better-smelling hombre than this."

I look at her in confusion, not sure if she's joking or not, but she doesn't give me a chance to respond.

"Captain's got a good plan there, don't you think?"

I nod slowly. "She does. It's probably our only shot at this. But it's pretty risky."

The woman smiles up at me from her place on the floor. "Nah, this ain't nothing, chico. You should have been with us when we fought those pirates or when the Captain and those big soldier types did that crazy space jump. We're all getting used to this sort of stuff by now."

Despite myself, I laugh lightly. "She really is something, isn't she? Now that she's finally become the captain."

The woman scoffs. "No, chico. She was *always* la Capitana. Everyone knew it; she just hadn't figured it out yet." With that, the green-haired woman gets up and walks away, going over to lean against the wall and talk to the big black guy who helped carry me onto the bridge. Quill...Quincy...Quinn, I think his name is. I laugh again as she passes by the stuffy Commander Illian on the way and smacks him on the butt, drawing a surprised yelp.

"Captain," calls out Illian as soon as he's recovered enough of himself to speak. "I'm sending the vectors to your implant now."

"Throw them up on the main screen," Lin says, "I want everyone to have a chance to look at them and give suggestions."

What follows is a beautifully orchestrated and *very* fast brainstorming session, in which Lin takes her already solid—albeit risky—plan and openly solicits suggestions from every person on the bridge, including me, that only make the plan better. Within two or three minutes, our approach seems just a little less insane, and I can see optimism in the eyes of every person on the bridge.

As for me, I still can't take my eyes off Jessica. At one point, she looks over at me and meets my gaze, throwing me a dazzling smile that makes my heart stop for a moment. The dual shock of seeing her alive and having her rescue me has me riding even higher than Kayla's truth serum.

Thoughts of Kayla and truth serum remind me both of the woman herself, sitting in *Persephone's* brig with the only other two mercenaries we know of who survived Jessica's assault on the station, and of Heather Kilgore, who is in the med bay being treated for her injuries by one of the enlisted women. I should be there with her, getting treatment for everything wrong with me after weeks of captivity and torture, but there's *nowhere* I would rather be at this moment than on this bridge watching Jessica work.

"All right, people," she finally calls out. "The time for adjustments to the plan is over. Now we execute. Commander Illian, fire on my mark."

## THIRTY-NINE
# RAZZLE DAZZLE

### *JESSICA LIN*

All eyes on the bridge are glued to the tactical plot on the forward viewscreen, where six ship-to-ship missiles are on a laser straight course from *Perse-phone* to the abandoned station. Six missiles for a station that small is a bit of overkill, but that's kind of the point.

I tear my eyes from the screen and look over at Brad again. He's not watching the plot with everyone else; he's still watching me. I've felt his eyes on me since the moment he stepped on the bridge. Surprisingly, it doesn't bother me. In fact, quite the opposite. I throw another smile his way, and he smiles back, and for that barest of an instant, everything feels wonderful.

It's with great reluctance that I turn back to the

tactical plot and watch as our plan hopefully comes together.

On the screen, the six missiles impact the station almost simultaneously, the difference in timing so small that our brains aren't even able to process it. Then, the plot shows a simulation of a large explosion—about what you would expect from hitting a small, unarmored station with *twice* the firepower required to destroy it.

"Chief Jensen, now!" I order, and the main drive ramps to full military power. I would hold my breath in anticipation of it possibly burning out, but at the same time, I'm pressed back into my chair as the inertial compensators and artificial gravity once again can't quite keep up with the sudden change in acceleration.

"Captain, *Brandenburg* just entered weapons range but hasn't fired yet," Illian reports in a relatively calm voice. He's a steady man under pressure, and I once again marvel at how much he's being wasted in a small system patrol fleet that doesn't even have ships to fly anymore. I wish I could have had a hundred of him in the Promethean Navy.

"The sensor scatter is working," I hear Lieutenant Robinson say in awe. "I can barely see them on sensors, and I know exactly where they are. But our change in acceleration means they don't have a location lock on us anymore."

I let go of a breath that I forgot I was holding and nod. By blowing up the station with a six-missile overkill, we created the equivalent of a large cloud of chaff between us and *Brandenburg*, effectively blinding the big ship's sensors for at least a few minutes. They'll continue to close the distance with us because they're carrying a much greater relative velocity to start, but the distraction might buy us just enough time to get to the second phase of our plan.

Not having anything constructive to do while we wait, I get up from my chair and walk over to where Brad is sitting. He goes to get up, but I wave him back down.

"How are you holding up?" I ask him in genuine concern.

He smiles. "Much better now. I can already tell I'm going to like the service here much better than my last accommodations."

A chuckle escapes my lips, and I shake my head at him ruefully. "You are something, Brad Mendoza."

He grins wider. "Charming, handsome, dashing, debonair, incredibly intelligent?"

I laugh again and wrinkle my nose at him. "Well, it's *something* for sure, but I'm not sure any of those words quite capture it. Smells like something else at least."

He laughs with me, and it's a good feeling. I can almost ignore the horrible stench coming off him; I wasn't joking about that at all.

Brad stops laughing first and looks at me soberly. "You're doing great, Captain. You belong in that chair. You always have."

I feel a hotness in my eyes that threatens more tears, so I just smile at him and shake my head. "Maybe I'm just keeping it warm for you."

To my surprise, he stops smiling. "No, Jess," Brad says in a very serious tone. "Now that I've seen you in the captain's chair, I would never take it away from you." Then he smirks mischievously. "Besides, assuming we can find what Kayla did with *Wanderer*, I won't be a captain anymore anyway. I'll be a *commodore*."

I snort—yep, really ladylike, but I simply don't care right now, and neither does Brad—and reach out one hand to give his shoulder a gentle shove. "Wonderful," I tell him, "I've created a monster. But I swear, if you go out and buy some silly hat, I'll shove you out the airlock myself."

He opens his mouth to give a riposte, but we're interrupted by Illian's voice.

"Captain, *Brandenburg* has reacquired sensor contact. They're painting us now with actives."

I give Brad a quick wink and then turn around and head back to my command chair. "How long to the horizon?" I ask.

"Five minutes and twenty-six seconds," reports Lieutenant Robinson. "It would be faster, but *Brandenburg's* angle of approach is not in our favor."

"We should disappear around the planet's curvature right about the same time that battleship can get a firing solution through the backscatter from the planet's surface," Illian confirms. "It's going to be close!"

Now, all we can do is wait. And the five minutes pass like hours as all of us are riveted on the tactical plot. Closer and closer comes the Jutzen battleship. With our higher acceleration, we're moving about as fast as they are now, but not directly away from them as we struggle to orbit the planet and get out of sight, while they inexorably close the gap between us.

Soon, we're down to thirty-two seconds, and suddenly, time starts to pass very quickly indeed.

"They have lock!" shouts Illian, his normally professional voice cracking. "They just launched a ship-killer and twelve ship-to-ships!"

I fight not to gasp. Similar to the barrage we launched at the station, Heinrich is taking the approach of massive overkill to deal with us. Well, no one has ever accused Nazis of being subtle. And the ship-killer shows he has *no* intention of taking prisoners.

I check the clock again. Eleven seconds.

Ten. The ship-killer missile behind us cuts its first-stage booster.

Nine. The missile's second stage kicks in, and with its now lighter mass, the massive nuclear warhead surges forward with renewed acceleration.

Eight. "Fire!" I yell, and two missiles from our meager stern tubes blast out toward the Jutzen battleship. It's like firing a bb gun at an elephant, for all the good those two little missiles will do, but it just seems wrong not to at least fire back.

Seven. The small rocky planet's gravity starts to bend our course further away from *Brandenburg*. I yell, "Fire!" a second time, and four interceptors join the two ship-to-ship missiles we just launched.

Six. Illian shouts, "Almost there!" with an odd note of excitement in his tone.

Five. Uvalde cries out in glee like someone riding an out-of-control horse for fun.

Four. The ship-killer's second stage drops.

Three. The big missile's third and final stage kicks in, blasting it forward so quickly that it looks on the plot more like a laser beam than a missile. If I thought Lawrence Poulter's ship-killer came at us fast, at this far closer range, the Jutzen missile makes it look like it was standing still.

Two. Proximity alarms sound, and the AI's robotic voice calls for us to brace and prepare for impact. Illian launches countermeasures without being told.

One. I hold my breath and say a prayer in my head. Just one word: 'Please'.

Zero. I look up at the plot as the dot representing the ship-killer merges with the one representing *Persephone* and all of us.

Nothing. No explosion. No nuclear fire. No instantaneous deconstitution of our atoms happening so fast that our brains can't even process our deaths. Nothing.

"It worked! The missile lost lock and got pulled off course by the planet's gravity before it could correct. It undershot us and its safeties kicked in when it hit atmo!" shouts Illian, and a cry of exultation rises from everyone on the bridge, myself included.

"We're over the horizon; *Brandenburg* can't see us anymore!" adds Robinson gleefully.

Then, the deck rocks beneath us as something explodes against our hull.

# FORTY
# LAST LEGS

### *BRAD MENDOZA*

The explosion jolts me against the restraints of my seat, and every bruise in my chest and stomach and all my broken ribs cry out in blinding pain, but I manage not to let the scream escape my lips.

"Report!" Lin shouts.

"Ship-killer missed us!" Illian replies. "But one of the ship-to-ships hit engineering!"

That's bad. We were all focused so much on the massive nuclear ship-killer that we pretty much forgot about the twelve smaller missiles the *Brandenburg* also launched after us. And apparently, one of those had a good enough lock on us to overcome our countermeasures and follow us around the planet's horizon and hit us where it hurts the most.

"Engines?" Lin asks, looking toward the enlisted man at the helm.

"Still running at full military power!" he shouts back. "But they're not responding to my commands, and I can't raise anyone in engineering!"

"Quinn, get down there!" Jessica shouts, and the big black man gets up from the place he fell on the deck and hurries out through the hatch, the dour woman named Heddy hot on his heels.

"Jensen," Jessica says next to the helmsman, "keep us on course for the slingshot maneuver. We'll use whatever the main drive is going to give us."

I pivot my seat and check the engineering display behind me. My heart sinks.

"Jessica—Captain," I call out, struggling to get enough air in my lungs to make my voice heard. "The main control conduit was severed right where it meets engineering. We've lost all engine control."

"Auxiliaries?" Illian asks.

I shake my head. "Everything is fried. It's possible you can reestablish local control...assuming there's still a console down there to do it with."

I hear Jessica swear, which is a rarity for her, but I get it. If we'd made a list of the worst things that could happen to derail our plan, this would have made the top three.

"How's the reactor?" she asks, trepidation in her voice.

It takes me a second to pull up the right display; I've never really worked an engineering console all that much before, and *Persephone's* Koratan interface is a new one for me overall. "Uh," I stammer, "looks stable."

There's a collective sigh of relief across the bridge. At least we won't have to worry about our ship blowing up on its own...probably.

"Captain," Quinn's somber baritone voice says over the bridge speakers. "I'm outside engineering."

"Can you get in and see if Jericho can ramp down the main drive?" Jessica asks.

"Sorry, Skipper," he replies. "The whole compartment is open to space and completely trashed. From what I can see through the one still-functioning camera, there are no survivors...or remaining control consoles."

A silence descends upon all of us as we contemplate the crewmembers we just lost. I never met a single one of them, yet I feel a melancholy tug at me that I know must be multiplied by a hundred for Jessica and the others who have served with the lost men and women for the last five weeks or, for some of them, much longer.

"Brad!" Jessica's sharp bark snaps me out of my reverie. "I need you to get down to the medbay and talk to Kilgore. I need something from her."

## FORTY-ONE
# ANOTHER DEATH CRY

### *BRAD MENDOZA*

"You're joking," a very upset-looking Heather Kilgore says to me as I support myself next to her med bay bed with the help of two women, Lieutenant Robinson and an older enlisted chief named Perry.

"Deadly serious," I reply. "It's time for you to come through on that whole 'I'm your best friend' thing. Because we need your help."

"You know that barely worked the first time you tried it, right?" she asks with a deep frown. "And it was one thing for *you* to transmit the Death Cry. It's a whole other thing for *me* to do it. There are…rules surrounding its use."

"Those rules won't matter a bit for you when we're all spare atoms floating in a cloud across this system,"

I argue back, using the closest thing I can muster right now to my old command tone. "Based on what I know of the Death Cry, this is the *perfect* time to use it."

Kilgore takes in a deep breath and then lets it out slowly. "Well, I guess I already gave away my King's biggest secret today. Let's go and piss him off even more."

I smile at her in gratitude and step back as the enlisted woman who's been treating her helps her sit up painfully in the bed and then assists her in hobbling after me and my minders to the bridge. I'm sure we make a sight: two dirty, bruised, and thoroughly odorous beings being helped to walk like small children.

"Agent Kilgore," Jessica says in greeting when we finally arrive on the bridge. "Thank you for doing this."

"My pleasure, I suppose, Captain," the Agent of the King's Cross replies, somehow knowing Jessica's new title despite being stuck in the med bay for the entirety of our desperate flight thus far. "And since we're breaking every protocol the King's Cross has already, is there anything in particular you'd like me to add to the message?"

"Now that you mention it," Jessica says with a wan smile, "while Brad and you were high on truth serum and swapping stories, did he ever tell you about the time he took out an entire pirate flotilla with one battle-cruiser?"

Kilgore looks over at me and sniffs. "No, he never got to that story. We spent most of the time talking about all the many stupid things he did as a kid and a midshipman. We didn't even have time to get to the *really* stupid things he's done as an officer."

Jessica smiles. "Well then, here's what I want you to say."

Ten minutes later, as *Persephone* leaves the small planet's orbit and we see *Brandenburg* doing the same not too far behind us, having followed us on our sling-shot maneuver, we have Kilgore's message recorded and ready. Robinson transmits it at a nod from Jessica.

"When will we know if it worked?" Kilgore whispers to me from where we're both sitting on the deck, propped up against the rear bulkhead in the increasingly crowded bridge.

"When we don't immediately die," I respond, throwing her a look.

So, we wait.

"Nothing yet," reports Illian. "We've been in missile range for sixty-four seconds, and they haven't launched. And they've got a perfect up-the-kilt shot on our drive nozzles."

I want to scream at him across the bridge not to jinx us, but that would be unprofessional.

"How long until we're out of range?" Jessica asks.

He shakes his head. "Assuming the main drive doesn't give out immediately, thirty-seven minutes."

Nothing more is said...really, there's nothing else *to* say, so we all settle down and wait. And if the five minutes we waited for *Persephone* to disappear around the planet's horizon felt like hours, then the next thirty-seven minutes feel like epochs.

Finally, Illian speaks again, breaking a silence that hangs over the bridge so thickly it makes it hard to breathe. "We're out of range, for now at least. But even a dip in the main drive and they'll catch right back up to us."

Again, what is it with this guy and jinxing us? I fully expect the drive to give out *right now* just because he said that!

"Then let's make sure we make the best use of the drive while we have it," Jessica answers calmly. She turns to Kilgore. "It appears our ruse worked. Between your death cry message letting them know the King's Cross will hunt them down ruthlessly and your intimation that there are Promethean warships already in this system, they appear to have hesitated just long enough to let us get away."

Heather Kilgore nods up at her. "Happy to help. Well, not really. I expect, as I'm sure you planned, that the real reason they actually didn't fire is so they can capture me alive and torture even more of the King's secrets out of me. Between this and the fact that I gave them the stellarium coordinates, King Charles is going to want my head, literally. But I guess I'm still happy to be alive, for now."

Jess smiles at her and then gives me a smile and a wink before she turns her command seat back around to keep studying the main tactical plot. I watch her every move. She's wearing a red and black leather getup that hugs her curves in all the right places. I love red on her. And her butt looks even more spectacular then ever!

"Get a room," Kilgore whispers so that only I can hear. I turn to her in surprise.

"I didn't know Agents of the King's Cross were allowed to have a sense of humor," I tell her.

She shrugs, wincing as doing so stretches bruised and battered muscles and possibly grinds together a few broken bones. "Oh, sure we do. It's important to lighten the mood with a joke or two when you're slitting the throat of an enemy to the Crown."

My jaw drops open in surprise and I stare at her for a while, trying to determine if she's serious or not. She smirks at me. "Stop looking at me like that. Jessica is right over there."

I shake my head and turn back to watch my former XO and the tactical plot in front of her.

# FORTY-TWO
# ULTIMATUM

### *JESSICA LIN*

"**M**a'am, we just lost the main drive," Chief Jensen reports unnecessarily. We all felt the jolt and the shudder through every deck plate as the engines finally gave out. It gave us almost a full hour *after* the missile hit engineering. It was far more than we could have hoped for but far less than we needed.

"Acknowledged," I respond simply. I'm not sure what else I can say right now.

Illian steps up next to me and speaks in a low voice. "Captain, we can't let that ship intercept and board us. Can you imagine what the Nazis would learn if they had unfettered access to two ex-Promethean senior officers and an Agent of the King's Cross? It would make

229

what Kayla got out of Mendoza and Kilgore a happy exchange of information by comparison."

He's right, and the mere thought of Brad back in the hands of those intent on torturing him isn't something I'm willing to even contemplate.

I turn and look toward the back of the bridge, not at Brad but at Quinn Boyd, who is lounging by the hatch. "Quinn, you still have some C8 on board?"

The big man shrugs. "I've got enough. Why? Want me to do a SOSO jump over to that battleship and blow it up for you?"

I smile despite myself because I really believe that, joking or not, the big man would do it just for the challenge.

"No," I tell him. "I have something else in mind." Then, I turn back to address everyone on the cramped bridge.

"Ladies and gentlemen," I say somberly. "It's been the highest honor of my life to serve with each and every one of you. But I'm afraid it's almost time to abandon ship. We have two objectives now, and only two. First, to escape the Jutzens. Second, to survive. I put them deliberately in that order. None of us wants to be a Nazi prisoner."

They stare back at me with equal parts despair in the situation and...hope in me. It's a humbling feeling seeing how they all automatically assume I'm going to get them out of this, and I almost find myself wilting under the pressure. But then I catch Brad's eye, and he throws me a jaunty smile and a wink to match mine from earlier, and it gives me just an extra measure of support to push forward.

"We're already on a course for Christos at good velocity and will arrive there in roughly three hours," I tell them. "My plan is to hold that battleship at bay long enough for us to get close to the planet so that our escape pods will be caught in its gravity. If we can make entry into the atmosphere, then *Brandenburg* won't be able to scoop up our pods. Once on the ground, you'll have to hide amongst the population in case they send troops down to search the surface. Hopefully, you all remember how to escape and evade from your SERE training. Lieutenant Uvalde will give each of you a rendezvous point in the capital city for one week from now. With any luck, we'll all meet then and have an incredible story to tell our friends and family one day."

No one smiles at my lame attempt to lighten the mood there at the end. Brad would have said something much more pithy, and even if it hadn't actually been funny, it would have made everyone laugh just because it came from Brad.

But for me, they all simply nod and look grimly determined, which I'll take. Because I don't want to lose a single person more than we already have on this mission.

"Captain, live message from *Brandenburg*," Lieutenant Robinson reports.

"On speaker," I tell her.

"This is Vizeadmiral Heinrich," a familiar voice says. "Do I have the honor of speaking with Lieutenant Commander Jessica Lin."

"No!" cries a voice from behind me before I can respond, and I turn to look at Brad in surprise. "You have the honor of speaking with *Captain* Jessica Lin of the Marauders!" he shouts.

I give him a confused look, and he just grins and shrugs. Marauders? Must be from one of those stupid mercenary books he's always prattling on about. Billy Firegoat...Firehand...Firebrand or something like that.

"My apologies," Heinrich sounds like he doesn't really care. "*Captain* Lin, I would like to discuss the terms of your surrender. I know you have lost your main drive, so I order you to fire your retro boosters and slow your ship. We will come alongside and render aid. You, Captain Mendoza, and Agent of the King's Cross Heather Kilgore will be our...guests, but we will let the rest of your crew go as a show of good faith."

I take a deep breath, taking one last look around me at the exceptional group of men and women who have somehow ended up under *my* command. I've been through more in the last weeks with these people than any other crew I've had the privilege to serve with. In each of their faces I find a hard resolve, and Illian shakes his head emphatically at me. Even Harris has wandered onto the bridge and throws me a look of encouragement and two thumbs up.

Then there's Brad. I look at him again, and from his eyes, I draw strength. Even if we could trust the Nazis, there is zero chance I will let them have him or anyone else under my command.

"That's funny, Vice Admiral," I say loudly. "Because we were just having a discussion on exactly where you can shove your terms."

There's stunned silence on the bridge and over the speakers. I look back at Brad to find him grinning widely at me and raising a single eyebrow. I actually laugh. Then I signal to Robinson to cut the connection before Heinrich can overcome his shock and reply.

"Commander Illian, I want you to start firing ship-to-ship missiles out of our stern tubes until we either run out of missiles or arrive at Christos. Let's not make this any easier for them than it has to be. If they get close enough, use the lasers."

# FORTY-THREE
## ENTRY

### *BRAD MENDOZA*

For three hours, Commander Illian keeps up a fairly steady barrage of two missiles aimed back toward Brandenburg every twenty minutes. It does no good as they easily swat them from the sky, but they don't fire back, no doubt planning just to catch us and board us as soon as we run out of missiles rather than destroy a potential intel win. It's not every day you get the opportunity to interrogate a King's Cross agent. Plus, their admiral *has* to be at least a little worried that there are other Promethean ships watching. Either way, he's closing the gap slowly but not launching his own missiles at us.

"Ma'am," the junior officer at the sensor station—

Robinson, I think—reports. "If we launch the pods in five minutes, we'll be close enough to Christos to be caught in the planet's gravity."

"Thank you, Lieutenant," Lin responds. Then she turns and regards everyone else again. "All of you, get to your escape pods. I will stay on the bridge to make sure nothing goes wrong and will follow in the last pod."

"With all due respect, Captain—" Illian starts to say, but she cuts him off with a hard glare.

"That's an order, Mr. Illian," she says in a command voice that makes mine look like a soft suggestion. It sends a little shiver down my spine.

"Yes, Skipper," he responds smartly. Then, everyone starts to file off the bridge. The enlisted woman from the med bay, who stayed silently in one corner of the bridge watching the fireworks after helping Kilgore here, returns and assists the red-haired assassin in standing and hobbling out through the hatch. The shooter named Heddy comes to me to do the same, but I waive her off.

Soon, it's only Jessica and me left on the bridge. She's still in her command chair, her back to me, and I watch as she reaches out and almost lovingly strokes one of the chair's arms.

"You never forget your first," I tell her, and she turns to regard me, though she doesn't look surprised at all that I'm still here with her. There are tears in her eyes, but her gaze is steady. Confident Lin, as I used to call the glimpses I would get of what she *could* be when faced with a problem to solve, is here to stay. I love it. Even the scars that cover one side of her face seem to enhance the effect, making her look like a warrior goddess from a video game I used to play as a kid. But I'm a little biased, I suppose, when it comes to Jessica Lin.

"I think you're right," she says in a low, husky voice full of emotion. "I wish I had more time with her. She's been a good little ship." She looks around. "Feels familiar, doesn't it?" she asks, referring to the last time she and I were alone on a ship we were about to abandon and blow up. Same name, too.

I painfully pull myself to my feet. She moves to get out of her chair and come help me, but I wave her off just like I did with Heddy. I hobble over until I'm standing next to her chair and reach out to support myself on its left arm.

"It's good to have you back, Brad," she says, her voice now barely a whisper as we watch the tactical plot still on the main viewscreen. It shows that *Brandenburg* is closing the gap rapidly now that we're out of missiles, but at least they still haven't launched their own. Apparently, they *really* want the chance to interrogate Kilgore, and I'm grateful they didn't find out she was a member of the King's Cross until *after* their last visit to the station. Besides, they probably feel secure with us fleeing back to the planet where they're obviously already welcome.

But they didn't count on one thing: they didn't count on Jessica Lin's resolve.

"It's good to be back," I tell her.

"About what you said on the station…" she says haltingly.

"Uh, yeah. Truth serum, right?" I say awkwardly.

"Of course, I'll understand if you don't feel the same way. It's a lot to spring on you right now with all of this. I mean..."

She reaches out and puts a finger on my lips, silencing me. "Brad, shut up," she says with a soft smile. "I love you too."

Well, we may be in the middle of a life-and-death situation, but fireworks just launched in my heart, angels now sing in my ears, and...half-goat men now dance in my stomach, or something like that. All I know is that if I die right this instant, I'm good.

We sit and stand there now in silence, watching the plot together, but she reaches out a hand and clasps mine in it, holding it tight as the AI's mechanical voice starts to report escape pods launching from across the ship. All will launch directly toward the planet's surface, with the exception of one. That one, which will carry just three passengers—Kayla and her two surviving crew members—will launch away from the planet to hopefully stay in orbit long enough for *Brandenburg* to pick it up. Having Kayla with us on the surface would just endanger all of us, and Jess and I could think of no better fate for her than to send her back to her business partners.

Jessica is still holding my hand a few moments later as she leads me off the bridge toward the last escape pod. There, at the hatch, she wrinkles her nose at me. "What, you think you get to ride with me?" she asks mischievously. "Do you know how terrible you smell?"

I laugh, but she shuts me up by standing on her toes and planting a gentle kiss on my lips through my scraggly beard.

Then we enter the pod, where we're still holding hands as it launches, and we watch through the rear display from a distance as the charges Quinn placed all around the ship light off, and our new *Persephone* goes out the same way our old one did, in a blaze of glory.

## FORTY-FOUR
# RENDEZVOUS

### *JESSICA LIN*

I walk into the small bar in what is certainly not the nicest part of Harrisburg, the capital city of Christos. I pause for a moment and let my eyes adjust to the gloom, but the bright purple—seriously, how did she find time to dye it a different color while on the run on an unfamiliar planet?—hair of Hayley Uvalde is hard to miss. Assuming she's going by Hayley again; one never can tell with her.

"Over here, boss!" she calls with a wave, and I make my way to the large round table, where I find Quinn already seated along with Illian, Perry, Heddy, and Kilgore. Even Harris is there, looking a little lost, as Harris always does.

I take the seat Uvalde indicates and turn to look

back at the open door to the outside. Brad's silhouette fills it, looking a lot better than it did a week ago—our fake identities as Ben Lopez and Jennifer Kim may not fool a single person in the galaxy, but they were enough to get Brad admitted to a real hospital here on the surface—and he looks around a bit before joining us, taking the seat next to me. I feel his hand reach out and grab mine under the table, and I can't help but smile as I study his profile. He actually looks pretty good now. He's no longer skin and bones, but he's nowhere near his original weight, either. The lost weight makes his face sharper, but it's a dashing look on him, especially without the scraggly beard. He still moves slowly, but he's recovering quicker than I expected.

"So, you too shacking up yet?" Uvalde asks.

I spear her with a shocked glare. "Uvalde!" I snap. "That's none of your business. Besides, Brad just got out of the hospital this morning."

The purple-haired woman grins and chuckles. "OK. But tell me you at least made out in the hospital bed, boss."

I can feel myself blushing furiously, and I raise a hand to hide my embarrassment. Brad answers for us. "Actually, if you must know, we're taking it slow. We've both been through a lot." It's partially true; we actually did make out quite a bit over the last week. At one point, we got his heart rate so high that the nurses came running. But they don't need to know all that.

"Sure you have, chico," the young woman scoffs. "But don't take it too slow, or she'll get away from you, sabes? Those scars make her look dangerous, and dangerous is hot."

Oh. Now I'm blushing so bad that Uvalde is really lucky I don't have a gun with me to take her out of my misery.

"Anyway," Brad changes the subject, falling into the strange role of being *my* XO. We discussed it while he was in the hospital—we had time on our hands when the Jutzens decided that it was more important to take their battleship and their new intel back to the Collective than stop at the planet and search for us—and, at least for now, Brad really wants me to keep being the captain.

"Has everyone checked in?" he asks. There are nods all around the table, and I breathe a long sigh of relief.

"Good," he says. "Any trouble with the locals?"

Quinn answers in his rumbling baritone. "Our pod took out a farmer's field outside the city. He wasn't too happy, but he calmed down a bit when Heddy worked her charms on him."

The dour woman smiles. "All I did was suggest that he and I wrestle. I've never seen a man run so fast away from a pretty woman."

There are laughs all around, and I finally find myself relaxing a little bit. But then I sober up because of what I have to say next.

"I'm not sure what happens now," I tell them honestly. I look at Quinn first. "I'm afraid you didn't get the loot I promised you. But we can work something out once Brad and I get back on our feet. Maybe…"

He waves it off. "You kidding, Captain? I got to kill Poulter's brother! I consider us even."

I smile gratefully, though I want to argue with him. He's being far too generous, but he gives me a little headshake when I open my mouth to protest, so I close it right back up.

Next, I look at Illian and Perry. "And without a ship, I'm afraid I don't have a way to get you and the rest of the crew home."

Illian shrugs, and Perry just smiles at me oddly. "Yeah, about that…" Illian says, looking over at Uvalde.

I follow his gaze and see my strange intelligence officer grinning rather broadly. "We've got a surprise for you, boss!"

Now, everyone at the table is grinning except for me and Brad. We just look confused.

## FORTY-FIVE
# HOME

### *BRAD MENDOZA*

I have no words. That strange little woman, Uvalde—she says her first name is Tina today—beams at Lin and me like a kid who brought home their first straight-A report card and was promised twenty credits for each A.

Heck, at this point, I'd give the purple-haired girl a few *thousand* credits if I had them.

"Uvalde, how?" Jessica asks in breathy amazement.

"It was no problema, boss," the woman replies, still grinning so wide it looks like it hurts. "Figured that tricky Kayla wasn't going to throw away a perfectly good ship. So, I did some asking around, and here she is!"

She's right. Here she is. Jessica and I stare in awe at

the not-so-sleek pregnant whale-like form of *Wanderer*, our little freighter, sitting on a landing pad at a small private spaceport outside Harrisburg.

"I don't know how to repay you, Hayley—I mean, Tina," Jessica says, uncharacteristically reaching out and enfolding the shorter woman in a tight hug as tears fall down her face.

"You'll think of something, boss," the woman replies cheerfully. "After all, we're going to be spending a lot of time together."

Jessica lets Uvalde go and looks down at her with a bemused expression. "We are?"

"De cierto!" the woman says. "What, you think that just because you rescue this hombre, you don't need an intelligence officer anymore?"

"Uh, I'm flattered you'd want to say with us, but we don't have any money to pay you," Jessica protests.

The smile on Uvalde's face doesn't even falter. "Oh, I'm sure we'll think of something to do about that, tambien."

"Actually," a deep baritone interrupts the conversation, "I have some ideas on ways we can earn some money."

Jessica and I turn to regard Quinn Boyd, who's making his way down the ladder from *Wanderer's* starboard airlock.

"Um, what were you doing on the ship?" I ask hesitantly. I really like Quinn so far, and Jessica seems to trust him completely, but it's hard to look at the guy without realizing he could break me in half almost by accident. He has really beefy forearms.

"Putting my stuff in my cabin, of course," the big

black man says as if I just asked a really stupid question.

"What?" Jessica asks.

Quinn shrugs. "Heddy's been my number two for way too long. It's time she runs a team of her own. I'm stepping away. Besides, I get so many more opportunities to blow stuff up when I'm around the Skipper."

I see Jessica blush, and she steps over and gives Quinn a hug equal to that she gave Uvalde. I see the big man's eyes tear up, but the look he shoots everyone over Jessica's head buried in his chest is enough that none of us mention it.

"We ready to go?" another voice intrudes. Seriously? How many more surprises are these people going to hit us with?

I turn to see Illian and Perry step up beside Uvalde. "Don't get me wrong, I love Carter's World," he says with a smile, "but one day, I'd like to command a truly great patrol fleet there, and to do that, I need experience *and* a way to get my hands on some ships. Hanging out with the two of you seems like it might give me both. If not, at least it won't be boring."

Jessica is speechless now, as am I.

"Perry is coming too," Illian says with a sly grin as the older woman smiles as well. "Said that someone has to make sure the Captain puts on that gross-smelling lotion."

Jessica guffaws aloud at this, but I just stare in confusion. I'm out of it for a few weeks, and these people already have inside jokes I'm not a part of.

"What about the rest of the crew?" Jess asks.

Illian shrugs. "They all wanted to go back to

Carter's World. Can't blame them. They found passage on a freighter bound roughly in that direction, leaving tomorrow. Robinson and Jensen will take good care of them."

I smile. At least that will give Jessica time to say a proper goodbye to her crew. I said a somewhat awkward goodbye to Heather Kilgore this morning. We actually invited her to come with us; a trio of fugitives from the Promethean Crown might have a better chance than just two of us. But despite her near certainty that King Charles will order her death, she still felt obligated to get back to Promethean space as quickly as possible to warn them about the Jutzen threat. She and I both expect them to move on Gerson as soon as Heinrich can get back to Collective space and rally a larger fleet, assuming he doesn't already have one hidden somewhere nearby, which is a real possibility.

"I guess we have enough cabins," Jessica is saying when I tune back in. "Illian can share with Quinn or Harris, and Perry can bunk with Uvalde. That leaves one extra bed if we need it. Speaking of which, where is Harris?"

"Uh, Captain," Illian says, sounding suddenly awkward. "That's all good for now, but we may need to rethink those living arrangements in the not-so-distant future."

Jessica gasps, and I follow her eyes to where Illian's hand now firmly grasps Uvalde's. "When did that happen?" she asks.

Uvalde shrugs. "Hombres find me irresistible. Poor Joe here didn't stand a chance."

"My first name isn't Joe," Illian protests, though there's no anger in it.

Uvalde rolls her eyes. "Your name is Joe today because today you're a Joe. Tomorrow, you might be a Todd, or a Gary, or maybe a Ulysses or Francisco. I don't make the rules, chico. But I always have wanted to kiss a Ulysses, so maybe…"

Their voices trail off as they walk away from us toward the airlock ladder, chatting the entire way and never letting go of each other's hands.

"I'll keep an eye on them, Captain," Perry says to Jess. I haven't spent a lot of time with the older enlisted woman, but she seems to have designated herself as mother and grandmother to Jessica, and I can't say that disappoints me. Lin needs all the support she can get in life, though she seems to be standing on her own rather well now.

"I'm sure you will, Chief," Jessica says. "I guess we ought to go aboard the ship as well and see what kind of mess Kayla and her mercenaries left us. And maybe find Harris."

"Harris is already on board," Perry says. "He just spent the last hour teaching me how to use some fancy anti-wrinkle cream. Apparently, I now have to do a seven-step skincare routine at the end of each day." The woman shudders visibly. "But, Captain, you have something else you need to do first." She has an evil glint in her eye as she holds up a bottle of what looks like lotion.

Jessica lets out a long sigh. "I thought Illian was joking. I assumed that all got destroyed with *Persephone*."

"Nope, I saved it all. Now, if you will?" the older woman holds out an arm to usher Jessica toward the ship, but reaches out a hand to stop me in my tracks when I try to follow.

"What?" I ask in confusion.

"Stay here, lover boy," Perry says with a smirk and a wink. "You don't get to see this yet."

And then they're gone, leaving me alone to stare up at my ship. Or is it Lin's ship? Is she still the captain now that we're back on *Wanderer*, or does it revert back to me? I look forward very much to discussing that and a myriad of other things with her in the days to come.

## FORTY-SIX
# EXES AND OH NO

### *BRAD MENDOZA*

"**D**ocking complete," Jessica says, sitting back in her co-pilot's seat in *Wanderer's* cockpit and throwing me a grin.

"Good job," I say, lifting my nose into the air and sniffing dramatically. Then, I mimic her upper-crust Promethean accent for the next part. "Keep that up, Commander, and you may have your own command someday."

She punches me in the shoulder. It feels great.

"So, freight?" she asks.

I sigh and nod. "Freight. It's boring, but at least it might pay the bills until we figure out our next move, so long as we can keep Quinn from trying to blow anything up that long. But hey, maybe we can catch a shipment to Carter's World. I hear you're some kind of celebrity there."

She laughs. "Sure. Just wait until the real President Carter gets his hands on *you*. They'll probably throw you a parade and make you give a speech."

It's my turn to laugh. We've been doing a lot of that in the two days since we left Christos and the Capaldi system behind. And kissing, we've been doing a lot of kissing. All of it is wonderful, and I can't remember the last time, if ever, that I've been this happy.

Actually, ecstatic is a more apt description. Every morning, I wake up expecting to find it was all a dream or that Lin has come to her senses and realized she can do *so* much better. But so far, none of that has happened. Maybe she really is crazy.

Jessica gets up and stretches, and I watch her do it. Trust me, you would, too. She yawns but tries to talk around it. "It'll be a race to see who finds us work first, you or Uvalde."

I snicker. I'd actually be a little worried about any kind of work Uvalde might find us. That girl has some weird ideas. I still can't wrap my head around how she and the stodgy Illian ended up an item.

Jess turns to go, and I watch her leave. She stops at the hatch and looks back at me with her eyebrows raised. "Captain Mendoza, are you staring at my butt again?"

I shrug and grin. "Guilty as charged, Captain Lin."

She gives me a fake scowl. "Careful, or I'll have you brought up for charges and keelhauled."

"I'm gonna risk it," I reply, and she laughs and then heads out into the corridor.

I take a few minutes to make sure that *Wanderer* is ready to switch over to station power, and then I get up and leave the cockpit myself.

When I arrive at the airlock, I find Quinn, Illian, Uvalde, Perry, *and* Jessica already waiting there. Harris arrives a moment after I do. Quinn bumps him with his arm, and they smile at each other. In perhaps the weirdest outcome of our whole recent adventure, the giant shooter and the taciturn and introverted makeup artist have become something approaching best friends. Go figure. I guess Quinn has had the guy endlessly customizing the uniform he made for him on *Persephone*. Harris even took my measurements to go make me some kind of uniform. I'm equal parts curious and terrified of what it might look like.

"Uh, Captain," Illian says, breaking my reverie as he peers at something on the small screen next to the airlock hatch. "There's someone already waiting for us outside."

I'm not sure if he's talking to me or Jess, but she answers first. "The authorities?"

"No, I don't think so," he says, scratching his head. "Looks civilian. A woman."

I shrug. "Oh well, let's go see what she wants. Maybe she's here to hire us."

Everyone chuckles a little at that. After what we've all been through, I think we pretty much collectively feel we can handle anything life throws at us now. Jessica and I move into the airlock, with Quinn following. He's our self-appointed security officer and bodyguard, and I can already tell he takes his job *very* seriously.

I open the outer hatch, exposing the station airlock on the other side, with both its hatches already open as well. There are bright lights that momentarily make my eyes water and obscure the woman waiting for us on the other end as just a silhouette in my sight. But there's something oddly familiar…

Holding Jessica by the hand, we walk through to the corridor beyond together so we can get a better view of our mysterious greeter.

I stop, my mouth falling open in shock, and all the air goes out of my lungs.

"Hi Brad," the pretty brunette woman says, then her eyes flash to where I'm holding Jessica's hand, and she lets go a little gasp of surprise. "We need to talk."

I still can't find my voice, so Jessica steps forward a bit. "And you are?" she asks coolly.

The woman in front of us blushes in a way that I remember all too vividly.

"I'm his wife. I'm Carla Mendoza."

# EPILOGUE

### *JESSICA LIN*

I've been walking on the clouds for the week and a half with Brad on Christos and then on *Wanderer*. At first, I was worried that finally telling him how I felt would open the floodgates, and things would move so quickly that I wouldn't be able to handle it. But surprisingly, Brad has been the one advocating that we take things slow. Maybe it's because he knows most of what's happened to me in my not-so-distant past. Or maybe it's just him being a gentleman. Either way, I find myself loving him even more than I did a week ago.

Which is really weird, considering how much he *annoyed* me, and even disgusted me, when we first met in Gerson. I'm still having trouble wrapping my head around it. But apparently love doesn't follow logic.

Besides, the thought of how my mother would react to learn I've fallen in with a simple farm boy-turned-officer from Denton III is almost enough on its own for me to keep things going.

Yes, everything has been just about perfect. Except for now. Now really sucks.

Because now, I'm sitting with Brad in a booth in a familiar bar on Hope Station, and sitting across from us is Carla Mendoza—no, Oliphant!—the woman who cheated on Brad and divorced him when he needed her most.

And that's not even the worst part. The worst part is the way Brad looks at her when he thinks I'm not watching. It's not the same way he looks at me. There's no passion in the gaze, but there is...something. I suppose that shouldn't surprise me—they were *married*, after all—but it still upsets me far more than it should.

Just my luck; I finally find a man I can be happy with, and his ex-wife shows up just *days* into the relationship!

"So, no one knows where they are," Carla is saying as Brad nods along. "They just disappeared, the entire task group. Without a trace. Not even Daddy has a clue where they might be, at least that he'll share with me."

Brad looks like he's going to say something, but I decide it's *my* turn to talk. "'Daddy' being Fleet Admiral Terrence Oliphant, the man who tried to destroy Brad's career?" I ask. I try to keep the cold, confrontational tone out of my voice, but I fail miserably. After all, Terrence Oliphant is also the man who *knew* I was being raped by Captain Jessup and Petty

Officer Nedrin Jacobs on the first *Persephone*. I may hate Brad's ex-father-in-law more than *he* does.

Carla frowns, and her eyes take on a defiant look in my direction for a moment, but then she looks at Brad as she blushes and nods. Oh…she's good.

"And the missing task group flag captain is Horace Clarington, the man you left Brad for?" I ask next, hoping this might throw her off a little more.

I feel a sharp pain in my ankle as Brad kicks me under the table. He is *so* going to pay for that later.

I can see the muscles in Carla's jaw tense in anger, but she nods again. Then she looks me dead in the eye. "Listen, Commander Lin, is it? I know that I hurt Brad, and I feel terrible about it. And I'm happy for the two of you and whatever this is you've got going on. I really am." She's really not; that's painfully obvious. "But I came here because he is the *only* person I could think of who might be able to help me. I cried for days when he was reported dead at Gerson, and when I heard rumors he might have survived, it was the best news I've had in a year. After all, I *was* married to him for six years."

She stops, an expression of challenge on her face as we stare at each other, neither of us even blinking. Volumes pass in those stares, and we both convey exactly how we feel about the other. But she looks away first. Having half my face covered in scar tissue has that effect on people. It's about the only benefit.

"Ahem," Brad clears his throat uncomfortably. "Listen, Carla, your dad has half the Navy under his command. Surely, he can—"

"No, Brad!" she snaps. "He can't because he and all of Second Fleet and half of First Fleet were sent to Gerson three weeks ago for who knows what. Whatever's going on out there, I guess a single missing task group is taking a back seat for now. So, my father can't help me."

"But Clarington's own father is a vice admiral. Are you telling me he isn't looking?"

She shrugs. "Horace and his dad don't exactly see eye to eye on most things. I can't even get the vice admiral to see me or take my calls. All I know is that four weeks ago, Horace and his entire task group were on their way to the Harper Line, but they never arrived there, and they never reported in."

Carla leans across the table and looks at Brad. "Horace isn't you, Brad. He tells me *everything*: where he's going, how long he'll be there, and he gets word to me if his plans change. But I haven't heard a single thing from him since he left. Except, maybe, for this."

She reaches into her stylish jacket and pulls out an old-fashioned piece of paper from an inner pocket, carefully unfolding it and smoothing out the creases almost reverently, then slides it across the table. Brad and I both read it, and our eyes go wide in surprise.

"I got this two weeks ago," Carla explains. "It's unsigned, but I *know* it's from Horace. Even so, I can't reach Daddy, and no one else will listen to me. So, I'm here, begging *you* to help me, Brad. You're my last hope. And if you still feel *anything* for me, like I still do for you, you'll help me."

Oh no. He's going to do it. By the look on Brad's face, it is *so* obvious that he can't say no to this terrible woman, and she's laying it on *thick*. Which means we're going to get embroiled in some other mess that's probably going to get us killed this time, for real. Stupid man! Why can't he just…

"Jess, what do you think?"

His question catches me completely off guard, and I turn to stare at him. Even Carla makes a little squeak of surprised anger that she quickly covers up with a fake cough.

By the look in his eyes, Brad isn't just asking me for the sake of saying he did, but because he *really* wants me to tell him what I think we should do. And I have the wonderful and also terrifying realization that if I tell him we should leave this alone, he'll do it! He trusts me that much. And the idiot probably won't even resent me for it later.

Which sucks double for me. Because him putting that much unconditional trust in me means that I have to answer him honestly; he deserves nothing less. I look down and re-read the very strange message his ex-wife got from *someone*, possibly from Captain Horace Clarington. And I sigh.

"I think we have to help her, Brad." There, I said it. I just agreed to help my new—whatever he is to me; we haven't exactly discussed that—help his ex-wife find her lover. It feels like an episode of a really bad daytime talk show, and I want to scream.

"But this note…" he says, almost in protest. "You know what this probably means?"

I nod and scowl. "Yes, Brad. I know. It means we have to go to the Harper Line and face the Koratans, and we're probably going to die in the process. What else is new?"

**THE END OF BOOK FOUR**

Want to explore more of the awesome universe of Dumb Luck and Dead Heroes? Pick up your copy of *Rogue Agent*, the backstory of Heather Kilgore, today on Kindle, Paperback, or Audible. It will help you enjoy the next book in this series, *The Worst Detectives in the Federation*, even more!

**HUNGRY FOR MORE?**

**SIGN UP FOR SKYLER'S NEWSLETTER AND STAY IN THE KNOW!**

Don't ever miss a new release!

Sign up now for Skyler's newsletter and get access to new release updates, free content, and great deals.

Just go to www.skylerramirez.com/join-the-club

# BOOKS BY SKYLER RAMIREZ

## DUMB LUCK AND DEAD HEROES

The Worst Ship in the Fleet

The Worst Spies in the Sector

The Worst Pirate Hunters in the Fringe

The Worst Rescuers in the Republic

The Worst Detectives in the Federation .

The Worst Traitors in the Confederacy

The Worst Fugitives in the Star Nation

The Worst Mercenaries in the Border Systems (Coming Soon)

## A STAR NATION IN PERIL

*Set in the same universe as Dumb Luck and Dead Heroes*

Rogue Agent

Suicide Mission

Assassin's Flight

## THE GALAXY'S WORST MERCENARIES

*Set in the same universe as Dumb Luck and Dead Heroes*

The Kaelen Extraction: A Billy Firebrand Adventure (Coming Soon)

## THE BRAD MENDOZA CHRONICLES

*Short stories in the same universe as Dumb Luck and Dead Heroes*

Saving the Academy

Battle for Poe

Siege of Jalisco

Death Station

Bells and Bullets

————

## THE FOUR WORLDS

The Four Worlds: The Truth

The Four Worlds: Subversion

The Four Worlds: Wrath of Mars

Ascension (Coming 2026)

Revolution: A Four Worlds Story

## ANTHOLOGIES

AI Apocalypse: A Collection of Science Fiction Stories (with Jonathan Yanez, Andrew Moriarty, Anthony J Melchiorri, and Stephen Gay)

## STANDALONE SHORT STORIES

Serena

# ABOUT THE AUTHOR

I just love writing. My goal is to write books that my readers enjoy and that celebrate everyday imperfect heroes. I want to show that everyone, no matter how life has dealt with them or how they've dealt with life, deserves a second chance and can go on to do amazing things. Just look at Brad and Jessica in Dumb Luck and Dead Heroes or Jinny Ambrosa and Tyrus Tyne in The Four Worlds.

It's important to me that everyone be able to read my books, including my teenage children, so I purposefully leave out any swearing or graphic scenes, though I don't shy away from serious topics. In this, I follow a tradition set by many (far better) writers before me, most notably in my life, Louis L'Amour.

As for the personal side, I live in Texas with my wife

and four children (and often a revolving door of exchange students), and I work for a major tech company in my spare time. But writing is my passion, and I often toil into the early hours of morning, especially on the weekends, and it's all worth it when I see people enjoy my books.

Thanks for reading!

Skyler Ramirez

amazon.com/author/Skyler-Ramirez

facebook.com/skylerramirezauthor

instagram.com/skyler.ramirez.author

tiktok.com/@skylerramirez_author

Made in United States
Orlando, FL
09 January 2026